An Hour of Need

A Shade of Vampire, Book 29

Bella Forrest

Also by Bella Forrest:

A SHADE OF VAMPIRE SERIES:

Series 1: Derek & Sofia's story:

A Shade of Vampire (Book 1)
A Shade of Blood (Book 2)
A Castle of Sand (Book 3)
A Shadow of Light (Book 4)
A Blaze of Sun (Book 5)
A Gate of Night (Book 6)
A Break of Day (Book 7)

Series 2: Rose & Caleb's story:

A Shade of Novak (Book 8)
A Bond of Blood (Book 9)
A Spell of Time (Book 10)
A Chase of Prey (Book 11)
A Shade of Doubt (Book 12)
A Turn of Tides (Book 13)
A Dawn of Strength (Book 14)
A Fall of Secrets (Book 15)
An End of Night (Book 16)

Series 3: Ben & River's story:

A Wind of Change (Book 17)
A Trail of Echoes (Book 18)
A Soldier of Shadows (Book 19)
A Hero of Realms (Book 20)
A Vial of Life (Book 21)

For an updated list of Bella's books,
please visit www.bellaforrest.net

Join my VIP email list and I'll personally send you an email reminder
as soon as my next book is out!
Click here to sign up: www.forrestbooks.com

Contents

PROLOGUE: BRUCELLA

After Sendira Mortclaw departed for the ogres' realm in search of her cub, I was left alone on Murther Island. Well, not exactly *alone*—the rest of the Mortclaws were still in their cave—but I decided to move away from the prison and put some distance between myself and those murderous creatures for a while, to allow myself time to clear my head after the encounter.

I waited and waited until Sendira finally returned with… bad news. She said that she had managed to find The Shade—or at least where she thought it was, based on the myriad of smells surrounding it. But on arrival,

Bastien's scent was far too weak. She'd concluded that Bastien definitely was not there, and must have left The Shade.

I cursed, wondering where on earth he could be if not The Shade. *Where would he have gone with that wench?* Then it struck me that together, they might have returned to The Woodlands. Where else would they have gone?

I instructed Sendira to search The Woodlands for the couple, in spite of my worry that she might snap up an innocent werewolf or two in the process.

When she returned this time, many hours later, she had a smile on her face—a smile that I couldn't recall seeing on her lips since before she and her family had been kidnapped by the black witches. She informed me that she had found her son in The Woodlands. She had picked up on his scent, soared over the land following it, and managed to track him down high up in a tree. She'd taken him away to a nearby rock formation where they could talk without interruption.

To my dismay, Sendira informed me that Victoria had *not* been there—or so Bastien had claimed. I drew in a sharp breath. This was definitely a setback. I still feared for my life every moment that Sendira was outside of that cave. My safety relied entirely on my shaky bluff, and her not wanting to risk that I was lying.

We couldn't just skip over the first task of ending Victoria and immediately launch into the second condition of our agreement. If Victoria was not taken out of the picture, Bastien would still be clinging to her in his mind. It would be hard enough for him to move on after her death, but knowledge that his little human still lived would make it a thousand times more difficult to ever get through to him, and for him to accept my daughter.

Victoria *had* to be eliminated before any marriage could take place.

Thus, as much as it killed me, it seemed that I had no other option than to wait. Hopefully not for too long. I'd witnessed with my own eyes how hopelessly infatuated Bastien was with the girl—I knew he could not stand to be parted from her for long. They would meet up sooner or later…

But I needed it to be sooner.

Very soon.

I did not want to enter a waiting game.

Hm.

Maybe, just maybe, there is a way for me to speed things up...

Chapter 1: Victoria

We were all in an utter frenzy over Grace's condition.

A *Bloodless.*

She had been bitten by a Bloodless and she was displaying the first symptoms of turning. After her initial fit on the bed, none of us were sure what to do. What we could do. Then Corrine, shellshocked as she was, took charge.

"P-Perhaps," she said in an unsteady voice, "Grace's tremors could be a symptom of something else. Please just… Let's not assume anything at all, until I have conducted a thorough examination. Dammit," she added to Grace beneath her breath, "I knew I should have done this as soon as you stepped in here."

She requested everyone leave the room except for River and Ben, who could hardly be expected to part from their daughter at a time like this. The rest of us piled out into the corridor, our stomachs tied up in knots.

Although we had been asked to leave, every single member of my family remained hovering outside the door, as if bound by invisible chains. But after an hour had passed, I found the wait unbearable. I kept mulling over and over the very worst-case scenario—that Grace's fae blood was not strong enough to counteract the Bloodless venom. That she was turning, slowly but surely.

As was usually the case in times like these, it was the uncertainty that wore us down the most.

I couldn't stand waiting outside the door any longer. I rose from the seat by my mother's side and stood up.

"I need some fresh air," I said to my parents, my voice raspy.

They nodded, and I took my leave. I had no idea how

much longer Corrine would take. I imagined that she was exploring absolutely every possible option before coming to her conclusion. As I made my way out of the hospital and into the flower meadow, the beauty of our island felt bittersweet. Almost taunting. I was close to Grace. Closer to her than many of the girls my own age. I loved her like a sister, and the thought of anything bad happening to her made me feel ill. But this… this was a level of bad that was practically incomprehensible.

I tried to force my mind onto more positive thoughts while winding my way through the sunflowers toward the woods. But it was a feeble attempt. There was no stopping my worry. The most I could do was walk and breathe deeply.

At least all would be clear after Corrine's diagnosis. We would know exactly where we stood.

I had almost reached the Sanctuary when a voice called behind me. "Hey, Victoria!"

I turned to find myself face-to-face with Brock Novalic. He stood on the forest path with a piece of parchment clasped in one hand.

"I just, uh, came from the hospital," he said.

"So you heard about Grace?"

"Yes," he replied grimly. "News is spreading quickly."

We fell quiet, gazing at each other as we both felt for our friend's plight. Then Brock cleared his throat. "The reason I came looking for you was… uh, I was by the beach about an hour or so ago, before I heard about what happened to Grace. And a message was delivered for you."

I knotted my brows. "A message? What do you mean?"

He handed me the parchment, upon which was scrawled a short note in black ink:

> *"Bastien wishes to see you about an urgent matter. Please return to The Woodlands as soon as you are able to.*
> *- Cecil"*

I stared at the note, reading it over several times. *Cecil? Bastien's counselor?*

"Wh-who delivered this note?" I stammered, gazing in utter confusion at Brock.

"A woman pulled up in an old boat outside the border. She was in a hurry and, to be honest, I didn't get much of a look at her. Just noticed she had darkish hair… She simply asked me to give this note to you," he explained.

"And she left?" I asked.

"Yes," he replied.

I blew out, glancing down at the note. This was strange. This was very, very strange. Was Bastien in trouble? Why would Cecil be sending me this note via some woman?

"Did she have straight hair?" I asked.

Brock squinted, as if dredging his memory. That wasn't exactly a difficult thing to remember about someone, but then again, Brock was a guy… "No," he replied after a pause. "She had curly hair."

Curly. Well, that definitely ruled Brucella out. Her hair was straight, not to mention lightish brown. I was sure there was at least one female member of the Blackhall tribe who had curly dark hair, though… She could have been delivering the note on behalf of Cecil, who was, after all, quite elderly.

Hm…

"Well," Brock said, sucking in a breath. "I need to get

going. I'll see you around…"

"Yeah." My eyes fixed again on the note.

I still couldn't shake my doubts about it. What trouble could Bastien possibly be in that *I*, a mere human girl, could help him out of? Unless he was assuming that I'd bring help with me, from The Shade. Dip into our pool of supernatural creatures.

The question continued to nag at me… *What if Bastien really does need me?*

Chapter 2: Ben

As River and I stood by our daughter's bedside with Corrine, I prayed harder than I had ever prayed before.

Please, don't let this be happening.

Don't let this be.

The death of a child was something a parent could never, ever recover from, no matter what the circumstances of their death was. But like this? I couldn't think of a more hellish punishment. I would rather spend the rest of my life in The Underworld than lose my daughter like this. And there was nothing I could do. Neither I, Lucas nor Kailyn were "true" fae like Sherus.

We were byproducts. We didn't possess the ability to turn others into fae—not to mention the fact that Grace would need to shed her physical body and become a ghost first, in order for adopting the form of a fae to be even conceivably possible.

Corrine refused to say a word to any of us as she moved about examining Grace: checking various parts of her body, prodding her with odd witch-crafted equipment, and feeding her various colorful substances. The methods she used were a mystery to us, and we were forced to sit quietly and watch.

I tried to hide my fear from our daughter, and I could tell that River was too. Though neither of us could think of much to say to comfort Grace in any way. As much as we tried, we were both simply too tense ourselves.

I wasn't sure what exactly the witch was thinking, but I already suspected her conclusion. It would be far too much of a coincidence for Grace's tremors to be caused by anything other than Bloodless venom. Was Corrine honestly hoping that they were the result of some kind of post-traumatic symptoms?

I couldn't believe it.

My eyes fell on the puncture marks in Grace's leg. And then my mind fixated on one thing: the document I had glimpsed on Atticus's laptop.

"Fight for Open Education on the Bloodless Antidote."
FOEBA.

Thank God that I had entered Atticus' room to see that. In this dark hour, that single headline of white text was my only glimmer of light, my only shimmer of hope that a cure did exist. Somebody must have discovered it, otherwise there would be no need for "Open Education" about it, and why were the hunters fighting so hard to suppress it?

We just had to find out what it was.

Grace is going to be okay. She's going to be. She's a fighter. She's a Novak.

I was already picturing myself hurtling back across the ocean toward the IBSI's base in Chicago to hunt down that laptop and swipe it. Wherever it was now, I would do whatever it took to get my hands on that information.

I waited another half an hour, which was what Corrine estimated it would take to complete her examination of Grace.

I could already tell from Corrine's expression what her conclusion would be as she took a step back from the bedside. Her face stricken with worry, she looked from me to River. She swallowed hard and shook her head.

"I've checked for every other disease and illness I can possibly think of that could bring about a violent reaction like Grace just displayed." She clasped her hands together. "I…" She averted her eyes to Grace. "Honey, I don't know what to say."

Grace looked paler than a spirit as she sat up on the bed, clutching the blankets to her in fright. I wished I could take away all of her fears and carry them on my own shoulders. I wished she didn't have to go through any of this.

River trembled next to me. I reached for her and Grace's hands, holding them as steadily as I could before clearing my throat. "Well," I said, my voice gravelly, "at least we know of a cure."

Grace stared back at me. "But we don't… We don't know of anything."

"We know of the *existence* of a cure," I corrected myself firmly. "It's clearly what Georgina died fighting to expose to the world. Somehow, I have to get hold of Atticus's computer. The details must be on those files, or the IBSI would not be so hell-bent on guarding them."

I rose to my feet and leaned over Grace on the bed. I brushed my fingers against her cold, pale cheek. Pressing my lips against her forehead, I cupped her face in my hands. I looked down at her steadily, forcing assurance and confidence into my expression.

"I'm returning to Chicago."

Chapter 3: Grace

My father didn't delay his departure in order to go outside and inform the others of Corrine's conclusion, or to fetch Kailyn or Lucas to assist him. He thinned himself and left instantly, leaving Corrine, my mother and me sitting in deathly silence.

My brain still hadn't quite accepted what was happening to me. But my emotions had. Fear gripped me so tightly, I was breathing like an asthma patient.

My mother moved close to me and placed a palm over my forehead. There was nothing she could say to ease my nerves. Nothing she could do. I might as well be all alone in the room. It felt like I was on an island all of my own right now, unreachable to everyone. Unhelpable.

Dad has to find those cracked files.

At least the tremors had stopped. I prayed that they would not return for a while.

"We should probably tell the others…" I croaked.

My mother nodded, her expression strained. She looked far older than her years right now. She headed to the opposite end of the room and opened the door. My family immediately rushed forward and began inquiring about Corrine's findings. My mother's expression should have been enough of an answer for them.

"I'm certain that Grace is infected," Corrine said quietly.

She might as well have announced that I had died already from their reactions. My grandmother Nadia burst into tears—hardly making me feel any better about my predicament—while the others looked utterly terrified.

"Ben just left for Chicago," my mother explained in a hushed tone. "He's gone to search for the FOEBA files that he spotted on Atticus' laptop."

I couldn't take the way everybody was staring at me any longer. I didn't want to feel like a dying patient. Not yet.

I pushed myself off the bed, and stood up. "I'm going to see Orlando," I announced.

Nobody argued with me or tried to stop me as I padded out of the room on shaky legs. I shut the door behind me, closing them inside.

Leaning my head back against the door, I breathed in deep.

I'm still alive. My heart is still beating. My brain is still functioning. I am still me. And my father has gone to search for the FOEBA files.

I ought not panic yet.

I fought to focus my attention on Orlando. I wasn't sure exactly which room Arwen had taken him to. He'd still been unconscious when she'd vanished him from my room hours ago.

I moved down the corridor, knocking on doors and inquiring who was in there, until Orlando's hoarse voice answered me.

I entered his room to find him alone in bed. He wore

hospital pajamas and looked *a lot* cleaner than when I'd last seen him. His shoulder had been bound with a thick bandage. He propped himself up on his elbows and gazed at me as I approached his bed.

"Grace," he murmured.

I realized that in this well-lit hospital room, it was the first time I'd ever seen him beneath proper light. Everywhere we had been together in Chicago had been so gloomy. Even during the daytime, heavy black-gray clouds had covered the sun, keeping the city in perpetual dimness, and there'd been no electricity—we'd used gas lanterns indoors, which hardly let off a generous amount of light. I took a seat by his side, examining his face. He looked a lot different with clean skin. Younger, for sure. Less worn and... less like an escaped murderer. His heavy-set brows looked less severe, as did his sharp features.

"How are you feeling?" I asked, my voice several tones deeper than it ought to be.

"My shoulder is all right, if that's what you mean," he muttered.

I nodded, pursing my lips. We had just lost his sister.

What else could he be feeling right now other than devastation? And he didn't even know yet about my father's suspicion that Maura had been turned into a Bloodless. He didn't know anything about what my father had witnessed within the walls of that crematorium.

I averted my eyes to my lap and twined my fingers nervously. I figured that I ought to tell him, no matter how painful it would be. It didn't seem right to keep that sort of information from him.

"After you fell unconscious," I began tentatively, "my father arrived. He is a fae, as I mentioned before—"

"I know that your father arrived and that he got me out of there, and the girl who woke me said he couldn't find my sister," Orlando cut me off.

"Right," I said, tense. "There, uh, was one other thing that I'm guessing she didn't tell you. My father witnessed the IBSI forcibly turning convicts into Bloodless… He suspects that Maura was a victim."

Wincing internally, I raised my eyes to meet his. He just stared back at me blankly, stunned. It took almost a minute for him to ask the obvious question. "W-Why would they do that?"

"We're not sure yet." I explained to him about what FOEBA stood for, and how the IBSI was apparently trying to wipe out all traces of its existence. I tried to reassure him that Maura might not be completely lost yet—that we might still discover the antidote. And I realized as I spoke that I was trying to reassure myself more than him.

I couldn't bring myself to tell Orlando what Corrine had discovered about me yet. I had come in here to see him in an attempt to distract myself from my own problems.

His voice caught in his throat. Shock gave way to grief, and then anger. White-hot anger. He leapt from his bed and stalked across the room. He raised his fists and brought them down against the wall, his upper back hunched and his chest heaving.

"Those people are the devil's doing," he hissed. "They all need to be lined up in a row and shot, dammit!" His voice cracked. "Before I die, I want to see them brought down, Grace. I want to bring them down."

I gulped.

I hope you'll have time.

And I hope I will, too.

Chapter 4: Grace

It took Orlando a while to sit down again. He continued pacing about the room, and I decided to stay with him a bit longer. Somehow I felt more comfortable in here with him than outside with my worrying family. Perhaps because he was also facing death.

I was glad that my family respected my desire for space, too, and didn't insist on hovering around me.

Orlando cursed and seethed until he seemed to tire himself out. He sank back into bed and drew up his knees, dropping his head against them.

I wasn't sure how long I sat with him—time had lost all

meaning to me—but when we were stirred by a knock at the door, I guessed that quite some time had passed… time during which I ought to be grateful I had not had another seizure. I hurried to the door and opened it to find my father standing before me. I immediately searched his face for signs of victory, but found none. His expression was stiff.

"I didn't find Atticus," he said, cutting to the chase. My stomach dropped. At least he hadn't delayed the pain. He took one of the seats in the corner of the room and sat down, gesturing that I sit next to him. My mother followed him into the room and stood between us, and I glimpsed the rest of my family gazing at us through the open doorway.

"I also could not locate his laptop," my father went on, "nor did I find any other accessible computer. I *did*, however, find something else that I know can help us in one of his desk drawers."

My father reached into his pocket and drew out a piece of paper. He unfolded it to reveal words in dark blue ink:

"Suspected FOEBA Involvement:
Georgina Conway
Deirdre Mighton

Roderick Gladwell

Frans Sanderson"

Beneath each of the names—except for Georgina's—were listed addresses: one in Sweden, one in Spain, one in Bermuda.

And then a final line was scrawled on the paper:

Hotel Brundbar, Sweden—Planned demonstration center.

I read the piece of paper over several times while Orlando peered down at it over my shoulder. I raised my eyes to my father. "So these must have been Georgina's accomplices," I said in a hushed tone. "And... 'planned demonstration center'..." My voice trailed off.

"Given that it's a hotel," my father said, "it sounds like they had been calling for a secret convention—I guess to demonstrate the antidote." His eyes grew wider with optimism. "You realize what this would mean, don't you, Grace?" he pressed. "It would mean that they must have had something very solid in order to demonstrate in the first place."

"Right," I breathed, attempting to allow my father's optimism to roll over me. "They must have."

"And we have addresses now. I'm going to leave right away to visit the first name on the list—Deirdre. And I checked the location of the hotel on the map already, it's not far from Deirdre's. I suspect that I can visit both within a matter of hours."

"Don't say 'I,'" I told my father, frowning. "I want to come with you this time. I can't sit around here any longer or I will go mad."

"And I will come, too," Orlando said.

My father exchanged a glance with my mother. Reluctantly, the two of them nodded.

"Of course I understand that," my father said. "All right. You can come."

After that, every single member of my family waiting in the corridor volunteered to accompany us.

"We should also take Ibrahim with us," my father said. "A warlock might come in handy. And a jinni too. I could ask Horatio."

And so it was decided; we would leave within the hour.

We're going to pick up where Georgina left off. We're going to take up her fight. The fight she lost her life for...

Chapter 5: Grace

My parents returned to our penthouse to fetch me some things for the journey—several fresh sets of clothes and my toiletry bag. I also requested them to bring me a pen and my pink polka-dot notebook, in case there was something I needed to take note of. I had to be alert to every clue we might come across.

After my parents returned and handed me some clothes—since I was still wearing a hospital gown—I changed before heading back to Orlando's room to see if he was ready. He was locked in the bathroom when I arrived. I sank down on his bed and pulled out the notebook while I waited. My chest twinged as I paged past the notes I had taken on Lawrence while I was his caregiver.

Orlando soon emerged from the bathroom, fully dressed in new clothes given to him, I assumed, by one of the hospital nurses. He wore extra-warm clothes, like those my mother had given me. She had even gone to the extent of providing me with thermal leggings, which I couldn't help but appreciate. Even while inside the building, it felt like it was all I could do to retain my body heat. As much as I tried not to think about it, it felt like my temperature was dropping slightly every hour.

Orlando seated himself next to me on the mattress, stealing a glance at my notebook. I shut it and stowed it in the mesh side pocket of my backpack. Some things felt too private for an onlooker to behold...

We were just waiting now for the rest of our party to gather in the corridor, probably within the next five or ten minutes. Then we would all be ready to leave.

I slanted a look at Orlando's face. He was frowning. "I don't understand why you people are so invested in finding the antidote. You people, here on your perfect island, away from the mess of the outside world… I guess what I'm asking is, why do you even bother?"

One answer to this, of course, was that we did care about what went on in the world outside of The Shade. Our island, as isolated and protected as it was, was still part of Earth. But, since Orlando would find out soon enough anyway, and I wanted to be completely honest, I decided now was the moment to just tell him. "Those Bloodless who bit into me in the sewage tunnel… They infected me."

Orlando's eyes bulged. "A-Are you serious?"

I nodded painfully. "I'm already starting to show signs of turning… Your sister was right. I might be half fae, but I am also half human."

He fell into chilled silence before asking, "Why didn't you tell me?"

"It's not exactly something I want to talk about, if you know what I mean," I said tightly.

He nodded. "Right." He continued staring at me, his eyes roaming from my face down the length of my body to my toes, and then back up again. "Well, I… I'm so sorry. I suppose that we really are in this together now."

"Yeah," I replied weakly.

The thought had already struck me that maybe, just maybe, this elusive antidote could possibly work on Orlando, too. We still had no idea exactly what drug the IBSI had given him to mess up his system the way it had… but I figured there was a strong possibility that his symptoms had something to do with Bloodless DNA. The idea didn't seem to be too much of a stretch of the imagination, given the scene in the laboratory my father had witnessed back in Chicago. The IBSI were obviously experimenting with them somehow.

I voiced this idea to Orlando. He responded with skepticism, though not hopelessness.

"Who knows," he muttered.

"All right, everyone," my father called from the corridor. "We're all here."

Orlando and I lifted ourselves off the mattress and hurried out into the hallway.

We all gathered in a circle: my mother, father, aunts Rose and Dafne, uncles Caleb and Jamil, grandpa Derek, grandma Sofia, great-grandpa Aiden, great-uncles Lucas and Xavier, along with my great-aunt Vivienne, Orlando and me. None of them wanted to be left behind on this mission. And in the center stood Horatio and Ibrahim. My father had apparently already given our first destination to the magic-wielders, and almost before I could blink, the hospital around us disappeared.

***

Sweden was definitely not the best place for a turning Bloodless to visit—especially not at this time of year. I gritted my teeth, gathering my coat closer around me. I caught Orlando shivering, too.

My mother, thoughtful as always, pulled out a lighter from her back pocket and handed it to me.

"Thanks," I said, quickly taking the lighter and sparking up a flame. I billowed it until it was a ball in my hands and moved closer to Orlando, allowing him to share its halo of warmth.

We were standing in the center of an icy road, surrounded by a world of rolling snow-blanketed fields. We appeared to be in the middle of the countryside. We crossed to the other side of the road and passed through a wall of trees, behind which we were met with a picket fence and a gate. Passing through it, we found ourselves approaching an old, rickety farmhouse. Just a brief glance at its derelict state—its broken windows and damaged roof—told me that nobody had lived here for a long, long time.

"This is supposed to be Deirdre's address, right?" I said, hit by yet another swell of disappointment.

My father nodded, sharing my sentiment. Though it wasn't like we had any excuse to be surprised. After what had happened to Georgina, we would have been surprised if we found any of the people listed on Atticus' note still alive and residing at those addresses. I supposed what we hoped to find was some kind of clue left behind. We were grasping at straws here, and any kind of clue that could lead us on the right trail would be helpful, no matter how small.

The farmhouse's rotting doorway opened easily— beneath just a light kick from my grandfather Derek. We entered a rundown living room, which probably had once been cozy, with its generous hearth and thick carpets— now covered with dirt and dust.

It was only a small farmhouse—two-bedrooms—and it didn't take long for us to search it. We looked beneath carpets, inside closets, between pillowcases. Heck, we even tore open the mattresses to see if there was anything we could find. But we found nothing here of note. I'd held out some hope about the bookshelf I had spotted in the kitchen, but after Rose, Orlando and I had flipped through every single page, we found nothing that could help us. Just recipe books for food. Not antidotes.

"I think it's time we admit there's nothing here," Lucas muttered.

"I agree," Derek replied.

My father sighed. "All right. We'll head to the hotel next."

***

The hotel was also situated deep in the countryside. It was an off-white building of five stories, much wider than it was tall. In front of it stretched a gravel parking lot, which was mostly empty. Apparently this wasn't the busy season. A glass-doored entrance emitted a warm orange glow, above which read a proud sign:

Brundbar Hotel.

I realized what an odd bunch we were as we moved to the entrance. Though, given the cold, I guessed that the paleness of the vampires among us would be easier to pass off.

We set our focus on the long oak desk at the end of the cheerfully lit reception room. A man sporting a smart black suit and bow tie sat behind it.

My father suggested in a low tone that just a handful of us approach the desk, while the rest of us hung back. I of course clung to my father and followed him to the desk, while Orlando stuck by my side.

"Excuse me." My father cleared his throat.

The receptionist rose to his feet and offered us a pleasant smile. "How can I help?"

"I have a rather unusual query," my father said. "I don't know how far back you keep a record of bookings of your conference rooms, but I'm trying to find out details about a meeting that was booked here about thirteen years ago."

"Oh," the man murmured. "I'm sorry. I am certain

that we don't hold such records."

Well, this was a short visit.

"Thank you," my father said faintly, before we backed away from the desk.

We returned to the others, who had all overheard the conversation. We headed out the doors, back into the frigid atmosphere. The sudden drop in temperature caused my teeth to chatter and my whole body to break out in shivers.

As my mother and father and everyone else huddled in a circle to talk about our next destination, I huddled closer to Orlando—not that he could provide me with any warmth. This wind, it was treacherous. My hands had started shaking so badly that I struggled to even spark up my lighter.

Orlando, noticing my effort, reached for the lighter to spark it for me. But before he could, the trembling in my body intensified tenfold. The next thing I knew, I was shaking so violently I could no longer hold my own weight.

I slipped on the snow, feeling arms close around my waist at the last minute. My brain had entered a state of shock as a tremor, as strong and dreaded as the first I had experienced, claimed my body. I registered briefly that it was Orlando who had caught and was holding me before more tremors started wreaking havoc on my limbs. I was vaguely aware of Orlando yelling for the others, then I closed my eyes against the cold. Against what was happening. As warm as the clothes were that my mother had equipped me with, it seemed that the icy atmosphere had triggered something in my system.

The ground left me, and I experienced the sensation of being whizzed through the air.

The tremors subsided slowly. When I dared open my eyes again, we had landed on a sunny beach—by no means hot, but not nearly as cold as the landscape we had just left.

Gazing up into a pair of deep, concerned dark eyes, I realized that Orlando was still holding me against him. My parents and the rest of my family moved around us.

My mother clasped my forehead. "Grace," she said in a pained voice. "You should go back to The Shade. This journey is no place for you."

"No," I wheezed. She didn't understand. I just

couldn't go back and wait blindly for their return. It would feel like I was just waiting to die. As shaken as my limbs still were, I fought to stand on my own two feet, with Orlando aiding the process—gently easing me upright. I remained clutching his arm.

A glistening sea stretched out before us. I drew in harrowing breaths, filling my lungs with the salty air, before managing, "We just need to keep moving."

Chapter 6: Victoria

After Grace and a few others decided to leave the island on their mission—including my parents—I bade them farewell with wishes of good luck. Then I was left to my own puzzled thoughts again.

The note from "Cecil" Brock had handed me was still in my pocket. I drew it out again and eyed it.

I ought to visit, I couldn't help but feel. *Just briefly to see what's going on.* There was no harm in that. I could ask one of the jinn to come with me—in fact, I was pretty sure that Aisha had stayed behind this time. She was a badass. I would be safe with her.

I took my bike and sped along the forest path toward the mountains. Leaving my bike outside, I passed through the entrance of the Black Heights that led to the jinn's apartments. I hurried to Aisha's door and knocked. The door opened after a minute. She emerged wearing a tank top rolled halfway up her torso to expose her belly. I took in her rather odd appearance before saying, "Aisha, I'm sorry to disturb you, but… I kind of need some help."

"That's okay," she said, in a surprisingly light mood considering everything that was going on around us. "Come in and chat, Victoria."

I stepped into her and Horatio's ornate foyer, and she led me into their beautiful sitting room.

I was just about to begin when she exclaimed, "I'm pregnant."

I forgot what I was about to say for a moment and stared at her. "Seriously?"

"Yes," she said, "Horatio and I… Well, we've been trying for a while actually."

"That's… Congratulations!" I said, managing to bring a smile to my tight, worried lips.

"Thank you," she replied. She remained beaming for several more moments before her face turned businesslike. "So, why have you come to visit me?"

I hesitated. Now that Aisha had told me she was pregnant, I didn't feel like asking her to accompany me. I thought I should ask someone else.

"It's, um… oh, never mind."

"Huh? What do you mean? Come on."

I heaved a sigh. "It's just that I received a note." I handed her the parchment, allowing her to read it for herself.

"Bastien," she muttered. "Your wolf boy, right?"

I nodded weakly. "Yeah… I was going to ask you if you wouldn't mind escorting me to The Woodlands, but—"

"I don't mind," she replied.

"Really? I mean, I would only plan a quick visit. It's just to see what's going on there, but—"

"I don't mind," she repeated. "I assume you want to leave as soon as possible, then?"

"Yes, but—"

"Then I'll get changed."

She left the sitting room and headed toward her bedroom. She returned less than ten minutes later, wearing a blue blouse and with her hair wound up in a severe bun on top of her head. That was usually her preferred hairstyle when she went to battle. It was Aisha's no-nonsense look.

"Thank you," I said, relenting.

***

We traveled via the gate in the ogres' realm to The Woodlands. On arriving outside the Blackhalls' mountain, I was hardly breathing. I gazed around the glade leading up to the entrance, and then at the wooden entrance door itself, looking for signs of struggle.

Everything seemed perfectly normal.

Aisha kept the two of us invisible just for good measure. I suggested that she vanish us inside rather than knock on the door. She transported us to the entrance hall on the other side. We ventured deeper into the mountain along the archaic corridors, and, looking around, all we saw were werewolves going about their day. Again, there appeared to be nothing wrong whatsoever.

We moved a bit further, but I didn't see a reason for us to continue remaining invisible. It also felt kind of rude and awkward to be trespassing in this manner. Aisha relinquished her magic and the two of us appeared before a group of werewolves who were heading toward us. They stopped abruptly, their faces lighting up in pleasant smiles as they recognized me.

"Victoria," they said, bowing their heads a tad. "You're back."

"Yes," I said uncertainly. "Is Bastien around?"

"Why, yes, he has returned from his trip. You will probably find him up in his quarters."

I thanked them and headed upstairs with Aisha. Although I still felt confused, a tingle of excitement ran down my spine at the thought of seeing Bastien again. At the thought of surprising him. I was already picturing the boyish grin that would spread across his handsome face, his arms around me... I knocked.

Footsteps...

The door opened.

And there he was. My wolf man. He wore sloppy

cotton pants and was bare-chested, since it was a warm day here in The Woodlands.

He immediately swooped down on me, gathering me to him and landing kisses on either side of my face and then my lips.

"Victoria." He beamed. His eyes flickered momentarily to Aisha. "How come you're back?"

"I'll, uh, wait outside here in the hallway," Aisha offered. "I trust you'll be all right…"

I looked at her gratefully. It was a sensitive gesture to offer us some privacy.

Bastien drew me into his quarters and pulled me to his sitting room, whose vast windows afforded a magnificent view of the fields bordering the mountain and the pure blue sky above.

"Tell me everything," he said, clutching my hands and gazing down into my eyes.

Relief billowed within me that he was all right, and apparently completely oblivious to any note. But this fact was at the same time very unsettling.

"Well, I received a note that was signed by Cecil. It said that you needed me and I should come back here as soon as possible."

His forehead lined in confusion. "A note from Cecil?"

"Some woman with dark curly hair delivered it," I added.

Bastien froze. Any relief I had felt instantly ebbed away.

"D-dark, curly hair? Did she have… gray eyes by any chance?" he inquired.

"I-I don't know," I stammered. "I didn't actually see her. A friend received the note on my behalf. Bastien, what is—?"

I didn't even have a chance to finish my sentence before a giant crash sounded just beside us, followed by a sprinkling of glass. Bastien and I staggered back, and the next thing I knew, we were standing face to face with a giant black wolf. She was about twice the size of even Bastien, who was by no means an average-sized wolf. She only just managed to stand up beneath the ceiling, which was hardly low.

"Mother?" Bastien gasped.

Mother?

What the…

Before I could attempt to make even the slightest sense of the situation, Bastien's body billowed and transformed into a wolf. He planted himself in front of me, blocking my view of the monster. "Call for your jinni," he hissed to me.

My voice was frozen in my throat, but Aisha must have heard the glass smashing. She came zooming inside within a matter of seconds. Her stunned expression mirrored my own as she gaped in the monster wolf's direction. *Bastien's "mother"?*

With the back of his leg, Bastien nudged me toward Aisha, who grabbed hold of me immediately. She put up some kind of swirling shield around the two of us—a protective shield, I could only assume.

From this angle, I had a clear view of the wolf. Her eyes flitted to me. Gray eyes—almost the exact same shade as Bastien's. She threw me a look of deep disdain before returning her focus to Bastien.

"Brucella has informed me that you have developed an unhealthy infatuation for this human." She spoke in a loud, booming voice. "It will not do. You are a Mortclaw, Bastien."

The hair lining Bastien's back prickled. "And who are *you*, exactly, to give me commands? You who only surfaced in my life a matter of days ago?"

To my surprise, the wolf's eyes softened as she gazed upon her son. *Really?*

"Please, do not fight me on this, child. I know that I am still a stranger to you. You may not understand now, but in time you will see that my actions are for the best…"

Her eyes returned to me and this time, to my shock, they were tinged red. Red that was growing more intense by the moment.

Either I or the world had gone mad when burning rays shot from her irises toward me. They sizzled up to three feet away from me, where Aisha's shield halted them abruptly.

Alarm registered in the wolf's eyes, and the rays instantly vanished. Then she leapt toward us. No, she *flew*.

Grabbing me by the waist, Aisha zoomed out of the window and positioned us in the sun-streaked sky. I hurriedly climbed onto the jinni's back as the wolf came hurtling after us. Claws the length of daggers extended from her paws, and she gnashed razor-sharp teeth.

I felt like I was going to pass out. Not even from fear, but from pure and utter bewilderment.

Aisha must've cast some invisible curse at the wolf, for she staggered in the air and faltered. It took her a few seconds to recover before she zoomed toward us again, and then again. Aisha kept beating her back with her magic, until it seemed that the wolf had given up.

She turned around and went racing right back toward Bastien, who was perched by the window gazing worriedly toward us.

What is she going to do now? Will she hurt him?

Aisha seemed to be posing the same questions to herself. She made us drift and follow her down. By the time we landed at the edge of the now upturned living room, it was to witness Bastien growling and gnashing in a corner as the giant wolf closed in on him. Within a matter of seconds, her jaws closed around the fur at the back of his neck, the way a cat would hold a kitten, and then… they vanished. Just. Vanished.

"Bastien!" I half screamed, half choked.

I gazed around the room helplessly, as if they would manifest again in some other part of the room.

That wolf vanished with him. And she had powers like that of the jinni or a... witch.

"What. Just. Happened?" Aisha breathed.

"I have no clue!" I cried. "She said that she was Bastien's mother. But Bastien's mother died! The hunters killed her! And what is a Mortclaw? Bastien's a Blackhall!" *Oh, God. Where has she taken him?*

Aisha remained speechless for several moments, simply eyeing the disheveled room. Then she wet her lower lip and turned to me. "I don't know what has happened here. Though the name Mortclaw does ring a vague bell. I think I have some inkling as to the cause of that wolf's powers, though it's kind of confounding why she would still possess them... If you want answers rather than my ramblings, I believe you need to speak to a black witch."

"A black witch?" I repeated, staring at her. "They were vanquished, like, ages ago. I don't know any..."

My voice trailed off as I realized that I did. *Of course I do, stupid.*

Mona. She had once been a black witch. A close companion of arguably the most notorious black warlock of all time, no less—Rhys Volkin.

Mona. We need to talk to Mona.

Chapter 7: Victoria

We returned to The Shade and, after gaining entrance to the island, Aisha took me directly to Mona and Kiev's treehouse. Mona came to the front door, looking surprised to see the two of us. I didn't think I had ever paid a visit to Mona specifically. In the past when I'd stopped by here, it was usually to see Brock about something.

"Victoria?" she said, her brows rising to her blonde bangs.

I was in too much of a rush to give her an introduction. "Do you know anything about the

Mortclaws?" I asked.

"Mortclaws," Mona repeated, mouthing the name with a look of wonder. She drew open the door wider and invited us inside. We took a seat with her around a cherrywood dining table. "Yes," she replied, to my relief. "Yes—they were the most virile tribe of werewolves in all of The Woodlands."

"And are you aware of any black witches meddling with them?" Aisha asked.

Mona nodded again. "I was never directly involved, but I heard of plans to experiment with them while I was part of Rhys' group. Morph the wolves into something nightmarish. Give them extraordinary powers that could match even a witch's..." Her forehead creased as she frowned. "What's this all about anyway?"

I hurriedly explained to her everything that Aisha and I had just witnessed.

It left Mona taken aback. "My, my... They still have their powers, all these years after the black witches' defeat," she mumbled, more to herself than to anyone else.

"The she-wolf told Bastien that he was her son—that

he is a Mortclaw, not a Blackhall," I said. "But how could it be? He doesn't possess the same powers as them... Well, he can shift at will from wolf to man. But he can't fly or vanish." *Or shoot freaking lasers from his eyes.* "And how is it that they still have their powers in the first place? And where do they live?" *I need to find Bastien!* It was bitterly ironic. Before Aisha and I had arrived in The Woodlands to check on him, Bastien had been fine. It was only after I'd acted on that note from "Cecil" claiming Bastien needed help that he really did need it.

I was throwing far too many questions at Mona at once, but I couldn't help myself. Every second that I sat here in this chair was torture as I imagined what was happening to Bastien. The she-wolf had mentioned Brucella. She was clearly behind all this. Knowing how crazy she was, and all that Bastien had told me about slighted werewolf mother-in-laws, I feared for his very life.

"Let's try to take this one step at a time," Mona said, rubbing her temples and focusing on the surface of the table in front of her. "Bastien. He might not possess the

Mortclaws' powers because, well… I really don't know exactly. I can only speculate that maybe the witches didn't experiment on him in the same way they did with his family. And, as for the Mortclaws still possessing their powers: Yes, it is odd, but… Not impossible. It depends a lot on the exact method the black witches used to carry out their ritual… As for where the Mortclaws live—I have no idea. Absolutely no idea."

But Brucella must know. She found them in the first place!

Oh, how I hated that woman's guts.

"So what do you mean by it not being impossible for the Mortclaws to have retained their powers?" Aisha queried. "How exactly would that be possible?"

Mona glanced at the jinni. "I have an idea… but I would need to go on a journey to verify it."

"A journey to where?" I asked.

Mona hesitated. She bit down her on her lower lip, as if she was having second thoughts. Then she replied in a far lower tone than usual:

"To a place I have fought for decades to forget."

Chapter 8: Bastien

As the giant wolf who called herself my mother shot with me over the waves, away from The Woodlands, away from Victoria, I shifted back into a man, hoping that it would help me break free from her grip. I transformed suddenly, and the idea worked. No longer covered in thick fur for her jaws to grip, I slipped through her wide jaws and went hurtling into a freefall down toward the ocean.

Colliding with the waves knocked all the breath out of me, but I did not have time to recover. I forced myself to swim deeper and deeper.

This isn't happening. This can't *be happening. What is this woman thinking?*

Ripples surrounded me, a disturbance in the water above me. I twisted my head upward for just a second and forced my eyes open to glimpse Sendira in the ocean. Still in her wolf form, it took her a matter of seconds to catch up with me, and then her body shrank and she resumed her humanoid form. I kicked hard to distance myself from her, but she grabbed my ankle, and the next thing I knew, the water around me disappeared and I was whizzing through the air again.

Oh, gods!

"Sendira!" I roared against the wind. I refused to call her Mother. She was no mother to me, no matter how much her scent drew me in. And she had lost all right to call me her son. She was no different than Brucella— cold, heartless, and merely out to put chains on me.

But Victoria had already freed me. She had freed my spirit and freed my heart. Nobody could put chains on me again, no matter how hard they tried. *I will not stand for it!*

"I promise that we will talk, Bastien," Sendira replied,

a hint of apology in her tone. "I promise. I just need to take you somewhere first."

"Tell me what is going on, now!" I bellowed so hard it felt I might have damaged my vocal cords. I expected her to just ignore me again, but to my relief, my sheer volume—and likely also the desperation rocking my voice—seemed to get through to her. She stopped zooming so fast and gradually slowed, until we caught sight of another random pile of rocks pushing up from the swelling ocean. Here she touched down with me.

My hands were shaking with anger as my feet hit solid ground. I backed away from her and glared at her.

In spite of my rage, I could not help but feel a bit taken aback on noticing how guilty she looked. This woman was a paradox to me. How could she be so vicious and hardened one moment as to attack the very woman her son had professed to love, and the next be gazing down at me with affection, the way only a mother could? It was unnerving. Endlessly unnerving.

"All right," she said, "I will tell you before we meet Brucella."

"Brucella!" I growled. "So you admit that she sent

you!"

She released a sigh and nodded. "Bastien, hear me out. Please, hear your mother out."

It grated at me to hear her call herself my mother. I wanted to correct her, spit out that she was no such thing, but her softened demeanor made me hold back.

She took my hand and held it in hers. "I was forced to make a deal with that wolf," she explained. "That deal is the only reason that I am free. She never would have released me from our prison if I had not agreed to her demands."

My head spun. "Wait. Release you from your *prison*? What? That's not the story you told me."

She swallowed. "I know. It pains me to say that... I lied to you." She proceeded to explain to me the full truth—she had not "just happened" to come across Brucella while roaming around the ogres' kingdom with my father; rather, they had been trapped for decades in a dungeon sealed off by the spell of a witch—the real truth of my family's history left me gasping for words.

"So... the deal," I managed. "What exactly was the deal?"

"Brucella demanded that we hunt down your human lover—who I must make clear, Bastien, is absolutely no match for you"—her softened expression turned hard again, but she continued before I could protest—"and then instruct you to marry Brucella's daughter, Rona."

I clenched my fists so hard, my nails dug into my palms. I'd just known that Brucella was behind this. I'd known it all along.

"I was supposed to take down the human just now," my mother went on, "but since she had that mystical being with her, I failed and had no choice but to take you away. It will be a waste of time trying to track that human down, and Brucella is unreasonable for suggesting it. So long as the human is protected by such a being, it is an impossible endeavor."

"And what were you planning to do with *me* now exactly?" I seethed.

"Take you to Brucella and inform her that I could not accomplish the first part of the deal—"

"But that you will attempt to force me to marry Rona?" I interjected.

She nodded, and then a scowl crossed her face. "That

bitch's daughter is no match for you either," she growled. "The only reason I acquiesced is because Brucella has assured me that she has a circle of witches who will immediately thrust me back into prison, should I step out of line."

I stared at her, disbelieving. "Do you honestly believe that?"

Her mouth twitched. "No," she replied. Then something sparked in her eyes—something dangerous, malevolent. "Why do you ask?" she queried me in a low tone.

"Because Brucella is lying through her teeth!" I spat. "She has no witches protecting her. She has nobody of the sort!"

Sendira studied my face for several moments. "I suspected as much. But we had no way of knowing for certain… *Are* you absolutely sure that she is lying? If you're wrong, it would be the end of us."

"I am as good as absolutely sure," I replied firmly.

A shadow descended behind Sendira's eyes, turning them from wintry slate to a stormy, blackish gray. A deep growl emanated from her throat as her body transformed into her monstrous wolf state. "Thank you, my dear. Now that you have freed me with this knowledge, Brucella will pay... A payment that has been decades in the making."

Chapter 9: Bastien

Sendira didn't utter another word as she transported me at heart-stopping speed across the ocean. We traveled so fast, I barely had time to speculate as to what, exactly, she had meant by making Brucella pay before she was already slowing again. Beneath us sprawled the grimmest landscape I'd ever laid eyes on in my life. A charcoal-black island that looked like it had been the casualty of a fire blazed up from Hell itself.

As Sendira descended with me toward a heap of giant boulders, I caught sight of a familiar figure pacing among the rocks. Brucella. I could have detected that wolf by her smell alone. My senses had been sharpened to her ever since I'd been on the run from her.

Sendira touched down several feet away from the woman, who immediately turned to us, an eager spark in her cruel, harsh eyes.

"I assume your first objective was success—" Brucella began, but Sendira gave her no chance to finish.

Without warning, my mother bolted for Brucella in her giant wolf form and pinned her to the ground. Everything happened at lightning speed. I could barely take it all in. One minute Brucella was screaming and pleading, and the next her cries gave way to... silence.

When Sendira stepped back and faced me, her jaws were dripping with blood. And within those jagged teeth was a still-beating heart. Her mouth clamped down, crushing the heart into a pulp. And then she *chewed*. *Chewed!* She was eating it! The organ of a fellow werewolf! I'd expected her to spit it out. Thrust it to the ground and roll it in the dust, maybe. But this... this was a level of horror my mind could barely even conceive. No werewolf did this to her own kind. I doubted even *Dane* would stoop that low.

My mother is a cannibal.

"Wha-What?" I spluttered, my brain too paralyzed to form a coherent sentence. As much as I despised Brucella, there was no part of me that had been prepared for this. *No* part of me. I couldn't even feel relief. Just utter shock.

Sendira finished chewing and swallowed with a deep, satisfied gulp. Then she swiveled and returned to the corpse. Before I could yell out, her jaws had closed around Brucella's right shoulder and she ripped out another chunk of her. She chewed again.

"Mother!" I rasped, forgetting to call her Sendira in my dazed state. I raced forward, placed my human arms around one of her forelegs and tugged at her, even as some of the blood staining her mouth speckled my arms. "What do you think you're doing?"

The she-wolf deftly brushed me aside. "Son," she managed through her mouthful, "I do not even remember the last time I ate. You can hardly expect me to refrain from tearing into a piece of meat when I see one."

"But that's not a piece of meat!" I panted, desperate

for her to stop. *I can't be descended from a family of cannibals, can I?*

What does that make me?

"Brucella is of your own kind!" I couldn't believe that I was even having to explain such a primal notion to this woman. "Even if you deemed her your enemy, you can't just eat her! That's… That's… I don't even know what kind of creature would stoop to this."

My words fell upon deaf ears. She finished swallowing her second portion of Brucella before her eyes fell on a large metal key with pointed teeth, lying on the ground near Brucella's head. "Aha," Sendira whispered. "There it is." She cleaned her soiled lips with her tongue before scooping up the key in her mouth.

"Come with me," she murmured through clenched jaws. "It is time for you to meet your *real* family."

I staggered forward, my knees shaky with sickness as I passed Brucella's mangled corpse.

Sendira led me over the boulders until we arrived at the entrance of a large, dark cave, closed off by some kind of fiery gate, secured with a dense iron lock. Sendira rushed to the entrance and fumbled to insert the key into the lock. She twisted to her right. The gate snapped open. It was as though she had just let a stampede of wild boar out of the pen. A horde of dark-furred wolves, as large and fierce as Sendira, all came shooting out at once and landed on the rocks surrounding us.

"We are free!" Sendira announced.

The group of wolves, who altogether appeared to be over fifty in number, formed a circle around Sendira and me, their focus first and foremost falling on myself. I looked at each of them with narrowed eyes, trying to comprehend who in the name of The Woodlands all these werewolves were. Then one of them stepped forward—a beast of a male, larger than Sendira. He stopped about three feet away from me and relinquished his wolf form, turning into a man as tall as me. He had earthy brown hair and eyes that were more gray-blue than my or my mother's.

He appeared aged—old enough to be my...

"Son." He spoke in a ragged voice.

Father...

This is my father?

He closed the remaining distance between us in a

flash. Planting his hands on my shoulders, he squeezed them tight as he gazed at me in wonderment. "Bastien, my child. It's you." His face, as hard and intimidating as it had looked just a few seconds ago, cracked and warmed with affection. His hands reached into my hair and he pressed his dry lips against my forehead.

I didn't know what to do. What to say. What to think.

It was impossible to describe the mélange of emotions coursing through my being in that moment. Shock. Confusion. Horror. Fear. Crushing disappointment. And a deep, almost unwanted, sense of nostalgia.

I recognized my father's scent too. Just not as quickly as I had Sendira's.

"We have much, much to catch up on," my father said, the corners of his eyes moistening. He looked like he could hardly believe his eyes.

"That is blood staining your lips." One of the wolves behind my father spoke up, his eyes trained on Sendira.

"Indeed it is," she replied with an expression of satisfaction. "There is some fresh meat beyond those boulders. But not enough to feed all of us."

My father's gaze turned savage at the mention of food.

As enraptured as he had seemed by me, he turned away and, after resuming his wolf form, led the pack over the boulders toward the corpse. I staggered after them with Sendira and could only watch as they ripped apart the rest of Brucella's body until there was nothing left of her but gnawed bone.

I drew in a deep breath, trying to keep myself from panicking. *Maybe I'm simply overreacting. They have been starving for decades. Is it really any wonder that they would be so desperate as to eat their own kind? I ought not be so quick to judge them. After all, it's not like there's any other food on this island…*

There hadn't been enough meat to go around. My father had taken his share first, and then he'd left the rest for the other pack members.

I was still staring at the skeleton when my parents approached me. "We must introduce you to your tribe," my mother said excitedly.

They proceeded to introduce me to numerous aunts and uncles, grandparents, nephews, cousins… They transformed into their humanoid forms as I greeted them, but my brain was in no state to retain many names, especially since my parents stopped only briefly by each one… except for one of my cousins, Yuraya. A tall, lithe girl with jet black hair, a sharp nose and narrow, ivy-green eyes. Older than me, according to my parents.

After listening to their prolonged introduction, I shook hands with her, perfunctory, and turned my back on everyone. I needed a moment of silence, of being alone, to try to piece together my shattered mind.

My knees finally giving in, I slumped down on a rock and dropped my head in my hands.

Oh, Victoria. I wish we could run away. Run away from everything and everyone, to a world where only you and I exist…

My mother disturbed my short reprieve. She sat down next to me and placed a hand on my shoulder. She glanced in Yuraya's direction, who had moved to the other end of the crowd and was talking to—if I remember correctly—her mother.

My mother dropped her voice to a hushed tone, and I scented the coppery smell of Brucella's blood on her tongue as she whispered close to my ear, "There is also something else that I ought to tell you about Yuraya."

She paused to give me a long, steely look, and somehow, I already knew exactly what she was about to say.

"She is your *true* betrothed, Bastien. Chosen for you by your *real* parents, ever since you were delivered from my womb. It is not Mortclaw tradition to encourage inbreeding, but… Yuraya is an exception. She is perfect for you in every way."

Now I understood the true reason for my mother's reluctance to my wedding Rona.

I hadn't thought that my world could come crashing down on me any more than it already had. But this was a final blow I could hardly stand.

Brucella was gone, and with her, her constant fight to rope me into marrying her daughter.

But now, with this terrifying revelation, I couldn't help but feel that Victoria and I had just leapt out of the frying pan and into the fire… A blazing, savage fire. The Mortclaws were a hundred times greater a threat than Brucella could ever hope to be.

"I'm in love with Victoria," I managed hoarsely.

My mother's hand pressed against my forearm. "So you have said," she replied stiffly. "But as I have explained, it will not do." She cleared her throat. "We will respect your past feelings for her, however, and will agree to not hunt her down, or harm her should we ever cross paths with her in the future... *if* you agree to never see her again."

Her words were a spear through my heart.

"You are already beyond your ripe age for marriage, Bastien," she ploughed on, "and once we return to The Woodlands, I expect your bond with Yuraya to be sealed within a week."

Nausea rolled through my stomach. It felt like the heavens had opened up and cast down a dozen leaden boulders to smash on top of me at once.

But perhaps my pain was self-inflicted.

Perhaps I was naïve to have ever thought that I could break free. Perhaps it was too much to ask for. Too much to dream of.

Perhaps I just ought to accept what every omen of destiny indicated that I remain.

A bird in a cage.

A beast in chains.

CHAPTER 10: VICTORIA

"To a place I have fought for decades to forget."

I had no idea what Mona meant by her cryptic response. After she clarified what she was talking about, I realized that we were about to embark on a journey to somewhere that had played a big part in her former, darker life, as well as her and Kiev's history. An island in the supernatural dimension that had once been central to the black witches' activities.

It was an island that used to be known colloquially as The Shade—a small version of our own island—because the witches had cast upon it a spell of darkness. Mona was sure that now, however, the island would look just like any other, that the sun would be touching it again. She suspected that the landscape would have become wild and overgrown, and the castle that had stood there derelict. But there was one part of the island that she believed would still be intact—the spell room, which was situated in an underground bunker. It was here that she guessed the bulk of the rituals involving the Mortclaws would've been conceived.

Mona said that she would go alone, but staying here on the island was my worst nightmare. The wait would drive me insane. At least if I went with her, I'd feel like I was moving. Like I was doing something. And I would not be left alone with my agonizing thoughts.

Aisha was also curious, but she said that she was feeling drained after the encounter with that giant she-wolf and thought she ought to rest. If Aisha hadn't been pregnant, that encounter wouldn't have tired her out so much. I thanked the jinni profusely for her help before she headed back to her apartment, leaving me with Mona.

After Mona agreed to bring me along, we traveled via

the gate in the ogres' realm again, since it was convenient. Here she grabbed my hands and vanished us again. When we reappeared this second time, we were standing on a rocky beach, a hard, blustering wind blowing against our backs. We had reached the shore of an island which was, as Mona had predicted, exposed to the sun and overgrown. She suspected that it had been left uninhabited all these years except by wild animals. It certainly looked like it as we ventured toward its center. The landscape was largely forested, and we found ourselves traipsing through dense undergrowth.

As the trees began to thin, I caught sight of a clearing which held a stone courtyard, behind which stood an old, towering castle with several shattered window panes. The crevices of its walls were stained with green—filled with moss and other weeds that had sprouted—and the roof was in thorough disrepair, with row upon row of broken tiles.

The castle possessed a creepy aura—my mind was already imagining what might be lurking within its dark, dusty halls—but at the same time, I couldn't help but admire its haunting beauty.

Mona's deep blue eyes lingered on the construction, a galaxy of memories behind her irises. She stood in silence for several minutes, just staring, until she drew in a deep breath and led me around to the back. We moved through a jungle of grass and weeds, close to the castle's anterior wall, until she stopped abruptly and knelt to the ground. She buried her hands into the growth of weeds and fumbled around. Her face scrunched in concentration. "The door is somewhere around here..." she muttered. "Aha. I've got it. Looks like it's open, too."

She gripped what I could now see was a metal handle and pulled upward. Hinges groaned and creaked as she pulled open an ancient trapdoor. Beneath it was a dark hole with a flight of blackened steps. She descended first and I followed closely, cautiously behind her. The sunlight trickled into the bunker in shafts, illuminating the cloud of dust particles we had unsettled during our entry. Through the gloom, I realized that this room was not all that different from Corrine's spell room in the Sanctuary, if more medieval. Countless rickety shelves were filled with bottles and liquids, and a rough wooden counter was dotted with cauldrons and stoves.

Mona stopped in the center of the room and gazed at the wall opposite us. Then her eyes lowered to a spot on the floor. She shook her head, grimacing. "So many memories," she murmured. "Kiev almost got killed in this room, you know. If I hadn't reached him in time, there would have been no Brock Novalic."

She lost herself in memories for a while longer, then snapped herself back to the present. "Right," she said, clasping her hands together. "Let me see what I can find in here..."

She began tackling cabinet after cabinet of potions, scanning every single shelf, before moving on to piles of wooden storage crates stacked up in one corner.

"Uh, what exactly are you looking for?" I couldn't help but ask. "I could help you."

"I honestly think it's best if you don't touch anything in here," she said, ignoring my first question.

Okay... I moved to the bottom of the staircase and planted my butt down on the lowest step. If I couldn't be of any assistance to her, at least I could stay out of her way.

I didn't say a word the whole time, not wanting to

disturb her concentration. Finally, she broke the silence and rose to her feet, clutching a large, bulbous-shaped vial in her hands, filled with thick, pale green liquid, tinged with brown. She moved toward a shaft of sunlight and held the vial aloft, twisting it back and forth and examining it. She nodded. "Yup. This seems to be it," she announced. "I guessed they would have stored it in here, if they decided to keep it at all. It's where they kept most of their experimental concoctions."

I rose to my feet and stared at it alongside her. "So…" I ventured again. "What exactly is this?" I still had not the slightest clue.

Mona glanced up at the trapdoor. With a flick of her wrist, it snapped shut, making me jump. I was expecting us to be plunged into complete darkness. But we weren't. The liquid in the vial… it was luminescent. It cast a pale green light around the room.

"This serum is still glowing," she said in a hushed tone, "which means that it is still potent… Now, for your question." She glanced up at me. "I believe that this serum is what is sustaining the powers that Rhys and his people imparted to the Mortclaws."

"Could you… explain how?"

She heaved a sigh. "Well, there is only so far that I can explain something as complex and twisted as a black witch's ritual. But I can say that the black witches had a kind of obsession with bonds and such—in case you couldn't tell from your family's history—since it was the ultimate exercise of control. All you really need to understand is that this serum is connected to the Mortclaws in a way I doubt even they are aware of. It would have been the potion they were forced to drink to seal their transformation, or in other words, the origin of their unnatural powers."

I was still feeling in the dark as to how this all worked. I knew that Mona was cagey about going into details of the black witches' heinous practices, because she had once taken part in them. Her past plagued her, even to this day. So I wasn't insensitive enough to press for more details, even though I was burning with curiosity. Mona had said she'd told me what I needed to know.

"So," I began, "what if we just… smashed this vial? If the Mortclaws' powers are connected to it, would those wolves be stripped of them?"

I might not have any idea where that she-wolf had taken Bastien, or what state he might possibly be in now, but the thought of that monster being stripped of her crazy powers while around him offered at least a bit of comfort. It would only help him in his situation, and he would be on more even ground if his own mother really did intend to harm him.

Mona hesitated. "You're right that it would strip them of their powers… just as it bestowed them. But it could also do quite a bit more than that."

"What?"

"You see," she said, lowering herself to a step and sitting down. She placed the vial on her lap and cradled it. "In order for their powers to have lasted for such a long time, they would have become practically part of their very being. Completely ingrained in their systems. They must have morphed to the point of no return. Anything less, and their powers should have faded by now. If we destroyed this potent serum, there's no saying exactly how it would affect them. It would be like ripping them apart… I suspect it might actually kill them."

I was wondering why Mona was talking as though that would be such a bad thing, when I realized... Bastien. He too had been affected at least in a small way by the black witches, in order for him to possess the power to shift at will. Might he be harmed, too?

"You're thinking that it could affect Bastien, even if he was touched only a little bit by the ritual?" I asked.

Mona shrugged. "It's possible. I was not there to witness the actual ritual, of course, so I don't know exactly how things came to pass. But I would advise that it's better to be safe than sorry."

Safe than sorry. And what was *safe* exactly? We weren't *safe* as things stood. Bastien had been abducted by a crazy wolf giant and was likely still in her clutches as we spoke. And yet... if we smashed this vial, and somehow, it did harm him...

No. I already knew that I didn't have it in me to take such a risk.

"Then what can I do?" I asked, swallowing back my disappointment. I'd really hoped that it would have been as simple as smashing this fragile glass of liquid.

Mona hesitated. She parted her lips, clearly about to

say something, but then clapped her mouth shut again.

"What?" I pressed.

She shook her head firmly. "It's not an option," she replied, clipped. "No idea why I even thought of it."

Clutching the vial, she rose to her feet. I gripped her arm.

"Please," I urged. "I'm open to any suggestion, no matter how stupid you think it is."

She drew away from me and headed to the stairs. "No, this was more than stupid. It was downright insane. And your parents would have my head for it." She flicked open the trap door, allowing the sun to spill through into the bunker again. "We should probably leave. I'm honestly not sure what can be done, unless you're willing to risk smashing the vial." She began moving up the staircase.

The reason for Mona's flightiness was clear. This room held uncomfortable memories. Still, I stood rooted to my spot. "I can't risk it... Would you have risked it, for Kiev?"

She stopped on the stairs. Her shoulders sagged. She shook her head. "No. Of course I wouldn't."

"Then won't you just tell me your other idea? Please."
I was begging now.

She clenched her jaw, her eyes falling to the vial clasped in her hands. Her grip tightened nervously around its sleek, glass neck. Then she returned her eyes to me.

"Victoria… How much do you really wish to be with Bastien?"

Chapter 11: Grace

After drinking some water and waiting a while longer to orient myself, I felt steady enough to let go of Orlando's arm and stand without anybody's help.

Our group traveled away from the beach and further toward the Spanish seaside town we'd arrived at. Europe wasn't plagued with quite as many supernatural problems as other parts of the world—though they were increasing day by day. There were still fairly large pockets of land where people were able to live normally. Looking around this quiet, sleepy town, it was clearly one of the lucky ones.

We stopped outside a residential block of apartments, four stories high. Not the most elegant of buildings, for sure. The exterior was shabby, with peeling paint and its lower walls plastered with graffiti.

We approached the intercom system. My father pressed the button for Roderick's door number, according to Atticus' note.

A woman answered, the crying of a baby blaring in the background. My father, who spoke fluent Spanish, told her that we had come to inquire about Roderick—whether he still lived here, or whether she knew anything about him at all. From what I could understand from her response, she informed us that she'd never known the man personally, but that he had died thirteen years ago from an overdose.

Thirteen years ago, just like Georgina. Now what a coincidence that is…

I wondered what kind of grisly death Deirdre had met with in her farmhouse. Of course, her death had probably also been covered up as either an accident or suicide. These hunters apparently would stop at nothing to conceal FOEBA.

"So," my great-grandfather Aiden said, as we moved away from the block. "Next is Bermuda."

Next and last...

"We're getting through the list quickly," Lucas remarked grimly.

Bermuda. We've got to find some answers in Bermuda. It frightened me to think that Bermuda might be another hopeless dead-end like Sweden and Spain. This list of names was all we had. We would be right back to square one if we didn't find anything at Frans' place.

Since there was a food stand on the other side of the road, my mother suggested that we stop for a bit and have me eat something solid. Orlando was probably hungry, too. Most of our party were vampires, but those who weren't, like my father, didn't eat anything. I didn't have any appetite, but I could only think that food would do me good, so I forced down a fresh sandwich, even though it tasted like cardboard. As Orlando ate his, I realized that I had forgotten to thank him for catching me.

"Thanks for earlier," I said.

He shrugged, not looking up. "I wasn't going to let

you fall, was I?" he said, swallowing.

"I guess not…"

I continued watching him while he finished his sandwich. There was something confusing… contrary about Orlando's character. Especially regarding his behavior toward me. *Every man for himself* had been his and Maura's mantra while they had been living in Bloodless Chicago—it was how they'd survived for so long in those dire conditions. But one way or another, with me, he always seemed to find excuses to make an exception to the rule, from the moment the siblings had found me in the tunnel and he had persuaded Maura to let me tag along, to persuading her not to rat me out to the IBSI after she had spied one of their "wanted" signs.

I thought back to the hour before my father had arrived to save me from the city. Just before Orlando had been sedated by a hunter, he had been on the verge of making a bargain with the IBSI. I'd never gotten a chance to hear what he had been planning to negotiate in exchange for his sister. But somehow, I couldn't shake the feeling that he had *not* been about to hand me over… Even though that would have made no logical sense at that time, since he'd had nothing left to lose.

I couldn't hold back the question now. "Orlando, what were you planning to offer the IBSI in exchange for your sister?"

Orlando swallowed his last mouthful of sandwich. His deep-set eyes flickered to mine, then away again. His hesitation gave me reason to think that perhaps I had assumed wrong after all. But then he replied, "Myself."

I scrutinized his thin, tired face. *Why would he do that when I was just around the corner?* And he had known for a fact that I was someone that the IBSI wanted—in exchange for me he could have even been offered treatment and release. He had been pushed past the brink of desperation at that point, I had seen it in his eyes. And yet still he had found an excuse for me.

"That makes no sense," I said.

He rolled up his plastic sandwich wrapping into a ball. Then he stood up, his tall, narrow form hovering over me. "It did to me," he replied simply.

With that, he turned his back on me and moved away to find a trashcan.

***

I didn't press Orlando further. I was left to my own speculations—not that I had long to mull them over. After the short breather we had taken for a snack, it was time to get a move on again to our next destination, Bermuda.

We gathered in a circle once again and prepared ourselves to hurtle through the air. We were traveling for just a few seconds before we once again felt sand beneath our feet. Only here, the atmosphere was much warmer and more humid. Still, I felt stuck in a refrigerator.

I opened my eyes. A crystal turquoise ocean licked the edges of a pure white sand beach. Before I could fully take in the beauty of our surroundings, however, my father led us across the sand—away from the water—and toward a line of drooping palm trees toward a road. We reached a pebble path which wound toward an old bungalow. Its painted green exterior was chipped, with missing slates on its roof. Stained red-checkered curtains concealed our view through the clouded glass windows. A large hive of bees had made their home right above the molded wooden porch.

Again, it was obvious that nobody lived here, not for

a long time. We all crammed inside and began to look around. The bungalow—which was really nothing more than a glorified beach hut—contained only four rooms in total: a single bedroom, a small sitting-cum-dining room, a kitchen, and a bathroom. Furniture was scarce, and what there was of it appeared eroded by time and dampness. A glass bookcase stood tall behind a rocking chair, by far the most interesting item in the hut. I estimated over fifty books sat on its shelves. Reaching it first, I creaked open the doors. As my eyes began running over each of the spines, my parents and Orlando joined me.

Clearly, Frans had been some sort of scientist—or at least taken a great interest in science. The topics of his books ranged from chemistry to physics to botany. The rest of my family joined us in taking a book each and paging through them, scouring them for anything that might indicate what the man had been doing while staying here.

The problem was, there were just *so many* books on so many different subjects that he really could have been researching anything at all. We found nothing to help guide us or draw any conclusions. Likely, there must've been some clues here at some point—like a pad of notes—but whatever pertinent information that might have once existed must have been removed by the IBSI. I wondered what excuse the hunters had fabricated for Frans' death. *Drowning in the ocean, perhaps.*

We exited the hut and descended the porch stairs before swiveling and gazing back up at it.

That was it.

Our last stop.

And, as I had feared all along, we had found nothing to help us. It clearly came as a heavy blow to my father. He was staring at the bungalow's door as if willing it to give up its secrets.

"Maybe I need to return to Chicago and just… wait for Atticus to return," my father murmured. "I mean, he's got to return there at some point…"

A mighty crash cut my father short. It had come from the direction of the beach, piercing the quiet atmosphere. It sounded oddly like the collision of wood. A lot of wood.

We all exchanged glances.

"What on earth was that?" Derek muttered.

Another crash. Then the groan of machinery.

Momentarily forgetting my father's suggestion, we all headed toward the noise. It called us away from the cluster of palm trees surrounding Frans' old hut and back to the beach. We followed the curve of the shoreline around a mound of rocks. On turning the corner, we came face to face with the source of the noise.

Three intimidatingly large black tractors were unloading piles of giant logs along an empty stretch of beach. The logs looked to be as much as ten feet in diameter. Behind the wood was more machinery—black towering cranes, which were gathering the logs and lifting them toward a pier, where a monstrous cargo ship floated.

"Does anybody else have the suspicion that the IBSI is somehow linked to this?" my father whispered.

The thought had crossed my mind, due to the black machinery. Everything about the IBSI was black, from their machines to their uniforms. Black to match their hearts.

We watched the tractors finish offloading their weight

before they trundled away over the sand toward a road.

"I'm going to follow them," my father said, already thinning himself and hurrying after them.

Ibrahim considered casting an invisibility spell over us while we waited, but that would make it more difficult for my father to find us. Instead we huddled closer to the rocks so that we were less visible to the suspected IBSI members further up the shore.

Thankfully, my father didn't keep us waiting long. He returned in less than two minutes.

"There's an IBSI base just nearby," he said. "It's just on the other side of the road."

"Hm." Grandpa Derek furrowed his brows. "I suspect this means Frans was definitely a member of the IBSI, for him to have lived so close. Maybe he was a scientist they had commissioned, or perhaps an advisor... or some kind of research assistant."

Ben shrugged. "Sounds likely... I didn't take the time to look around the base. I want to do that now. I suggest we all move a bit closer first."

My father led us away from the rocks, across the stretch of sand and into another gathering of trees until we arrived outside a gated compound. Surrounding it was a high fence, most definitely electrical. An off-puttingly sweet, nutty scent pervaded the area, quite unlike anything I'd smelt before.

We moved closer to the fence to peer through the small gaps, careful not to get too close. The usual brown tinted glass, oblong buildings were present, but there didn't seem to be many of them. In fact, this compound did not appear to be very large at all—at least not compared to Chicago. Clearly this wasn't one of their main bases but a small sub-branch.

The roaring of tractors sounded to our right, where the main entrance was located. They were coming out again. This time, however, they weren't filled up with logs but... leaves? Shockingly large, wide leaves with a strange peachy color. Their texture reminded me of aloe vera plants—the leaves looked smooth, bloated and squishy, like they were filled with some kind of liquid.

The tractors carted them back toward the beach, no doubt to be loaded onto that cargo ship, too, along with the logs.

"That's smoke in the distance," Orlando commented,

drawing everyone's attention away from the disappearing tractors. He was pointing to our far left. Indeed, a cloud of black smoke swirled overhead, somewhere behind the compound.

"Maybe another one of their laboratories," I said darkly.

"I'm going to take a proper look around now," my father said.

"I'm coming," Lucas said.

The two of them thinned and left the rest of us to wait again.

When they returned, about ten minutes later, I never would have predicted the first words that spilled from my father's mouth:

"They've got another portal here."

Chapter 12: Grace

"Another portal?" several of us gasped at once.

"Yep," Lucas said, crossing his arms over his chest and looking grim. "Another bloody portal."

"Leading to where?" Vivienne asked.

"We don't know," my father replied. "We didn't get that far yet."

"And what about all that smoke?" my mother asked anxiously. "Where is that coming from?"

"There's a huge pit round the back—they're burning those same type of logs and leaves we saw earlier."

"Burning?" Rose said. "They're both burning those

materials, and going to all the trouble of transporting them God knows where in that cargo ship? How does that make sense?"

My father and Lucas shrugged.

"The smell," I said, realization dawning on me. "That must be where that weird smell is coming from. From those trees."

"Is the portal within the compound itself?" Derek asked.

"No," my father replied. "It's just behind it. Though I'm sure that this whole area from the fence onward is prohibited."

"Well, if the portal is outside, at least it will be easier to check it out," Derek said.

I wasn't sure how any of this was relevant to our search for the antidote, but right now, it wasn't like we had anything else to do other than see where this trail led. My father's alternative suggestion had been for him to just hang around Chicago and wait for Atticus to return—but we had no idea when, or even if, that would happen. Or whether Atticus would still have the files accessible on his computer.

Derek turned to Ibrahim. "Can you move us all closer?" he requested of the warlock.

Ibrahim acquiesced, while Horatio transported himself. A couple of seconds later, we were standing on the other side of the cloud of smoke beneath a sparse line of trees.

My father led us ten feet forward and circled a wide, round bush. A dark hole came into view amid the undergrowth. An abyss. I was sure that this was the widest that I had ever laid eyes on—wide enough to fit at least fifteen full-grown ogres, I figured.

"I'm going to jump through first and see what's on the other side," my father said. He looked at us seriously. "Wait here until I return."

I held my breath as my father dove into the portal. He hurtled downward and quickly disappeared from view into the starry depths.

When my father returned, only about a minute later, I couldn't help but let out a breath. I was used to my father being the guinea pig for things—given that he was a fae, and arguably the least vulnerable of all of us due to the IBSI's ignorance of the species—but that didn't stop me from worrying about him.

His expression was stricken with shock as he came zooming out of the hole and returned to us. He was oddly out of breath as he stammered:

"It's… It's Aviary."

Chapter 13: Grace

Aviary.

To say that place had played a significant role in my father's history would be an understatement. He'd been kidnapped there as a baby, and that was where all his troubles had started—troubles that had plagued him in his later life, which were the reason he'd become a ghost to begin with, and why he was no longer in his vampire body, but that of a fae.

No wonder he looked shaken.

"Are you *sure* it was Aviary?" Grandma Sofia pressed.

"Yes," my father said, exhaling deeply. "I'd recognize

that place in the dark. I'm sure of it. The wild, Jurassic jungle, the suffocating heat, the penetrating humidity… it's Aviary."

"The Ageless was supposed to have closed all the portals to Aviary four decades ago," Ibrahim muttered. "I guess there were some she wasn't aware of."

"I didn't venture far, obviously," my father went on, "since I was barely gone a couple of minutes—but while I was gazing around I couldn't miss a wide trail that had been made in the undergrowth, right by the other end of the portal. It was heading into the thick of the jungle." He paused to take a deep breath. "Something tells me the IBSI has definitely set up some sort of base over there."

An IBSI base in Aviary. The concept left me unsettled. That the hunters' organization of today, which was an entirely different animal to the one that had been controlled by Hawks in my great-grandfather Aiden's time as a hunter, should come full circle and return here now… It was uncanny. Like it was returning to its roots, in a sense.

"So the portal doesn't emerge within an actual IBSI

base on the other side—you're sure of that, right?" my mother verified.

"Yes," my father replied.

As we all fell quiet for several moments, I suspected that we were all thinking the same thing. We were all curious now to travel through the portal and see what the IBSI was really doing on the other side.

If they did have a major setup there, this would not turn into another blitz like the League had inflicted on them in the Woodlands or The Trunchlands, of course. We weren't equipped for such a task, and that wasn't why we were here. Eradicating the IBSI from the supernatural dimension had dropped lower down on the League's list of priorities after my nasty Bloodless surprise. If we made a trip there now, it would be done out of pure curiosity and investigation.

"So… Do we go through?" Aiden posed. "What do you think, Derek?"

My grandfather still appeared to be considering the matter deeply. "Well," he said heavily, "a part of me is obviously reluctant to embark on what could very well turn into a wild-goose chase—a waste of our precious time, given Grace's predicament. But another part of me can't help but wonder if we were meant to stumble upon this. Frans' address was right on this place's doorstep…"

My grandfather's gut instinct mirrored my own. I moved to him and placed one hand over his, squeezing it. "Let's go through, Grandpa."

My father heaved a sigh. I knew how much he hated Aviary—the place was traumatic for him. And in a way, it was traumatic for Derek, Sofia and Aiden, too, all of whom had a less than pleasant history with the place.

Still, we all agreed.

My father set his eyes on me. "The heat might be living hell for the rest of us over there, but at least it won't be for you."

Chapter 14: Grace

In spite of my body's innate coldness, even I could sense the sharp rise in temperature. Worryingly, however, I did not feel the urge to peel off even a single one of my thermal layers. This temperature just made me feel comfortable rather than jittery.

Orlando, on the other hand, did remove his jacket. He slipped it down his shoulders and tied it firmly around his waist. I took this as a harrowing confirmation that I was further gone than him.

Oh, God. We have got to figure out the antidote!

Surrounding us was a world of gargantuan trees—

trees that were identical to those the IBSI had been burning back on Bermuda and transporting to the beach. Their fluid-filled peach-colored leaves hung heavy from the sturdy branches, creating a thick canopy above us that let only the occasional sliver of sunlight through. This was an advantage for the vampires, at least. A low humming of insects filled my ears, punctuated by the squawk of a bird or the growl of an animal I'd rather not picture.

I moved to the trunk closest to me and sniffed it. The bark emitted the same nutty smell I had noticed earlier, though it wasn't sweet. I supposed the sweet odor had come from the burning leaves.

As my father had already informed us, to our left was a wide track created by some kind of large machinery. Tanks, maybe even more tractors.

"Construction noises," Derek said. "You hear them?"

The vampires among us nodded. We were without an invisibility spell now so that we could keep an eye on each other.

"I guess let's see where it leads," Lucas said, already moving toward the track.

My father gripped my hand firmly as our group trudged forward to follow Lucas. The path appeared to extend for miles in an almost perfect straight line, surrounded on either side by the pinkish trees. To speed up our progress, and to decrease the likelihood of getting impeded by some wild animal, Ibrahim transported us several miles up the track by magic. Here, I heard the noises my grandfather had been referring to. The trundling of heavy machinery. The creaking of boughs. The occasional yell of a man. And sawing. Lots of sawing.

From here, I could just about make out the end of the track in the distance. It gave way to some kind of clearing, illuminated by sunlight. Magic transported us the rest of the way.

Reaching the bottom of the path, we found ourselves gazing around a vast open space—larger than I could ever have expected. The ground was a graveyard of trees. They had been felled for miles and miles to our left and right. Black cranes, tractors, and other machinery equipped with giant saws were lined up at the far end of the clearing, directly opposite us, where the jungle of pinkish-leaved trees began again.

I counted ten caravans littering the flattened area, where armed men and women in black uniform were apparently taking shifts. Some held mugs and packets of food, while others spoke into communication devices.

We backed up further into the shadows of the trees to avoid being noticed.

"What is it about these trees?" I breathed.

It was Orlando who answered. "You know," he whispered, his dark eyes wide as he beheld the massacre, "I can't help but think back to that shelf in Frans' hut... There were quite a few books on botany, weren't there?"

I hardly dared to think about what Orlando was implying.

Could it be? Could these trees have something to do with the antidote?

CHAPTER 15: GRACE

"Uh, we need to get out of the way," Caleb said suddenly, looking behind us. I couldn't see what he had noticed, but he had obviously heard something with his vampire ears.

"Sounds like more hunters are coming through the portal," my mother said.

"Let's head up into the trees," Horatio suggested.

Following Horatio's lead, Ibrahim transported us up into the tree tops. He settled us down along a branch that was so large all of us could comfortably stand… Well, as comfortably as you could stand, like a hundred feet above the ground, while surrounded by creepy-crawlies and God knew what else.

My aunt Rose had already spotted a monstrous spider, which just happened to be crawling near where she and Caleb had been planted. She clutched Caleb's arm hard. Caleb smirked, pulling her to stand on the other side of him so that he acted as a barrier. As brave as Rose was, she was still a little girl when it came to spiders. And crabs.

"Now we're closer," Ibrahim said beneath his breath, moving toward one of the squishy leaves surrounding us, "let's check these out…"

He slipped out a Swiss knife from his pocket and sliced off a sliver of the leaf's flesh. We all watched as the gooey substance within the leaf dribbled into Ibrahim's cupped right hand. In texture, the substance wasn't far off from the gel found in aloe vera, except this was tinged yellow and appeared more gooey.

"D-Do you think there's any way…" I began.

My voice trailed off as I stared at Ibrahim disemboweling the chunk of leaf. He poured the remaining runny gel-like substance into his hand, separating it from the skin.

He sniffed both the leaf and the fluid before replying, "I think it's possible. I mean, the way those hunters are working down there, it looks like they're trying to drive this tree into extinction. I do believe this species is native only to Aviary."

Although it would make sense, I still struggled to wrap my mind around how something so pedestrian as a tree could possibly have anything to do with curing the deadly Bloodless infection.

"The thing is," Ibrahim went on thoughtfully, "I'm not sure how we would test it. These leaves are obviously the most potent part of the tree, but they could very well be poisonous. I don't know what kind of effect they could have on a person's system."

I extended a hand to the yellow gel the warlock was holding.

"May I touch it?" I asked.

He nodded.

I dipped my finger into the substance—surprisingly cool—and brought it to my nose. Yes. This smelled sweet. An odd smell for something poisonous. I usually thought of poisonous things as bitter, sharp, or pungent to the nose in some way.

Then again, I wasn't exactly a botany professor.

Horatio also broke off a chunk from one of the leaves and examined it. "Hm. I'm afraid I don't have much to add to this conversation," he said. "I've never come across this type of tree before in my life. This is the first time I've ever visited Aviary."

Being born into a family of jinn royalty, I supposed that Horatio would have had no reason to visit Aviary.

I glanced back down at the film of yellow coating the tip of my forefinger. I was so tempted in that moment to taste it, to see what it did, if anything. *What's the worst that could happen? I'm dying anyway.*

"How about I try it?" Orlando spoke up behind me.

I whirled on him. "Huh? You?"

The rest of my family showed equal surprise.

"Yes," he replied, his jaw set. "Me. Given everything I've learned from you people since leaving Bloodless Chicago, I'm pretty damn sure that whatever those bastards did to me, I have some mild form of Bloodless DNA in my system that's made me so sick. I mean, look at me." His arms flanked his sides. "I even look like I'm in the process of turning, don't I?"

I bit down on my lower lip. Yes, he did. Though I didn't have the first clue what the hunters were hoping to achieve by messing with Bloodless in their drug development. They were supposed to be developing a drug that enhanced a person's strength and abilities, not turned them into sick, pale creatures like Orlando. Though, after witnessing Lawrence's transformation on TV, they had obviously finally gotten something right...

Before any of us could talk Orlando out of it, he reached out and tore off a chunk of leaf. He eyed it briefly before raising it to his lips and taking a bite. *A bite.* My insides squirmed as he chewed with an uncertain look on his face, then swallowed.

I stood with bated breath, waiting for what, exactly, none of us knew. But as Orlando broke out into a violent coughing fit—so consuming that he lost his footing on the branch and slipped—this had clearly been a terrible idea. "Orlando!" I gasped as my arms instinctively shot out to grab hold of him, but missed. Horatio zoomed toward him and caught him before he could fall too far down the tree. The jinni lifted a choking Orlando back to our level and stretched him out on the bark. He and Ibrahim hurriedly knelt over him. Orlando had started to wheeze like he was suffocating.

Ibrahim cursed, even as he flipped Orlando over so that he lay on his stomach. Then, without warning, Ibrahim levitated Orlando in the air and flipped him upside down. The warlock shook the young man vigorously, so vigorously I feared Orlando might even suffer a concussion. A retching sound blurted from Orlando's throat, followed by a stream of puke (which a part of me couldn't help but hope would land on a hunter's head).

Ibrahim continued to shake Orlando until it looked like he would start vomiting out his organs if he upchucked anymore. Then Ibrahim laid him back down on the branch before summoning a flask of water from his backpack. Ibrahim pried Orlando's jaws open and filled his mouth to the brim with water. Orlando choked and spluttered, but as he slowly sat up, he was breathing.

Orlando wheezed out a long breath.

"Thankfully," Ibrahim said, "I managed to catch most

of it before it could travel too far into you." The warlock grimaced and threw me a look. "So, Grace, I think we can safely conclude that these trees are poisonous."

My heart sank to my stomach. I returned my focus to Orlando. Poor guy. He was looking ill as death.

"So you really got it all out of his system?" I asked Ibrahim worriedly.

"There will still be traces of it, but it shouldn't be a lethal amount. Orlando, you're probably not going to be feeling too good for a while… It's just a good thing you had a snack earlier, or it wouldn't have been as easy to induce the vomiting."

Orlando's face was uncharacteristically flushed, I guessed where the blood had flooded to his head.

We all fell quiet, giving Orlando some moments of peace while he recovered. I found myself scrutinizing his face the whole time, watching the redness fade. After a couple of minutes, the blotchiness had gone, but bizarrely, he didn't look as pale to me as before. Maybe I was just clinging to a desperate hope, and it was clouding my vision. I could've sworn, though, that his complexion had brightened a touch.

"Hey, does anybody else notice this?" I called, narrowing my eyes on Orlando, still believing they were deceiving me.

"What?" Orlando and several of my family asked at once.

"He looks kind of… healthier?" I dared say.

Orlando was immediately surrounded by everyone ogling him like he was a rare specimen.

"Hm… Maybe just a little bit," my mother replied. "But that could still be the effect of the blood going to his head from all the shaking Ibrahim gave him."

We waited another five to ten minutes, during which time we continued to observe Orlando, who looked rather awkward beneath everyone's close scrutiny.

I kept expecting every moment for the slight warmth in his skin to fade, and return to its former pallid, lackluster state. But it didn't happen. Orlando was still pale, no doubt, but his complexion was closer to that of a naturally pale human than a… very *unnaturally* pale one.

"You guys see what I'm seeing?" I whispered.

"Yes," Derek replied.

Ibrahim's forehead wrinkled in a deep set frown. "This is… curious. Curious indeed."

"Should I eat more of the stuff?" Orlando wondered, even as he looked sickened by the thought.

"No," Ibrahim replied quickly.

"Why not?" Orlando asked.

"Because it was killing you," Ibrahim replied, exasperated. "I can now say with utmost certainty that this stuff is *not* supposed to be consumed neat. The effect it's had on you is interesting, though—of course, we will have to see if it lasts longer than an hour… But if these trees really have something to do with the antidote, then I suspect they are part of a more complex recipe. These alone would kill you well before they ever cured you."

"How do you really know that for sure though?" Orlando pressed.

Ibrahim widened his eyes. "Didn't it feel like it was killing you?"

"Yes," Orlando admitted.

Ibrahim blew out. "I mean," he said, rubbing a palm over his forehead, "as I said, this is not a species of tree that I have experience with. But I know enough about medicine to conclude with ninety-nine percent certainty that if I hadn't made you vomit when I did, you wouldn't be sitting upright now. In other words, I don't think it's wise to risk it."

"Then… if these trees are only part of the formula," my grandmother Sofia said, "I wonder what on earth the other ingredients are?"

Ibrahim stroked his dark goatee. "Hm. I would assume something powerful, yet non-toxic to the body, that could soften the effect of the tree's poison… No idea what exactly. But I could take a bunch of these leaves—and some bark for good measure—back to the Sanctuary to experiment on with the other witches. Maybe we can even figure this out without the IBSI's help…"

"That would be a blessing," I whispered. "But how long do you think it would take to figure out?"

"You know I can't answer that," Ibrahim replied. "It could be an hour, if one of us had an epiphany, it could be weeks… or it could be never, if we've got the wrong end of the stick entirely here."

I glanced at my parents. They looked conflicted.

"Well, Ibrahim," my father said, running a hand through his hair, "why don't you return and get started, at least. Gather as many witches as you can to help you and start working as fast as possible."

"I guess you'll need some Bloodless to experiment on?" my mother asked.

Ibrahim nodded grimly. "I'll have to pick some up on the way back home. Won't be too difficult, though. We will have to do our best not to kill any of the test subjects…"

The warlock moved about the branch, cutting off generous chunks of leaves as well as bark shavings. He filled his backpack until it was bursting at the seams. Then, giving us one final nod, he vanished himself back to the portal.

Our eyes roamed to Horatio—the only magic-wielder left among us now. He would need to take charge of transporting us places henceforward.

"It would be quite uncanny if these trees really could reverse the Bloodless infection," my great-grandfather Aiden said, running a palm along one of the smooth, broad leaves.

"What do you mean?" I asked him.

"Well, the Bloodless virus, or whatever you want to call it, is nothing but a mutation of the original vampirism introduced to humans by the Elders. As you know, Grace, from your history lessons, Aviary and Cruor were bitter enemies. I just think it would be oddly fitting if Aviary possessed a neutralizer."

"Right," I said, nodding slowly. I hadn't thought about it like that.

We fell quiet, each of us sinking into our thoughts. The noises of the hunters demolishing the jungle echoed up from beneath us.

If these trees were the answer, we couldn't have the IBSI felling them like this. I had no idea how widespread they were in Aviary. For all we knew, they might even be a rare species. If the hunters continued to work at this pace… How much longer would we have?

I exchanged an anxious glance with my father and mother.

"While Ibrahim is gone," my father said, addressing the group, "we have got to stop them from wiping out these trees."

Chapter 16: Grace

"We should damage their machinery," my father proposed.

"Or," Lucas posed, "we could fetch more recruits from The Shade and launch an all-out attack on them, Woodlands-style."

My father and grandfather looked hesitant.

"First of all," my father replied, "that sort of attack would destroy a lot of these trees—we're talking about dragons' fire here, Lucas," he reminded his uncle. "Secondly, a heavy-handed attack would likely send the hunters into a panic. Once alerted to our presence, they could start destroying the rest of the trees at a much more rapid pace. Maybe even bomb the whole area."

"But I wonder why they haven't done that already," my mother said.

"Well, they are clearly keeping aside a stock of these trees for themselves. But if worse came to worst, I imagine they would forfeit the option to collect more and instead just destroy everything here…. If we discreetly got to their machinery, for example later tonight after they have all finished work, that would definitely slow them down. I'm guessing it would take them a while to gather enough machines again to continue at their current pace. We'd be buying ourselves some time. And as long as they didn't see us here, they wouldn't suspect us. Nobody would know what had happened."

"I agree," Derek said. "We need to tread carefully here. Very carefully."

"I wonder if any of the hunters working here might have the recipe for the antidote," Xavier proposed. "I wonder if any of them have been told what they're doing here, or whether they're just blindly following their authorities."

The same question had arisen in my mind too. Something told me they were simply obedient workers who had been fed some other reason for why they needed to fell the trees. I doubted very much that Atticus had allowed the antidote recipe to be made common knowledge within his organization. I figured that most IBSI members were probably not even aware of an antidote. As Mr. Munston had told me back in Chicago headquarters, FOEBA was classified information.

"I doubt it," I said.

"Though anything's possible," my father went on. "After we have messed with their machinery tonight—and checked for any explosives in their possession—Lucas and I could spy on their camp and see if we can overhear anything relevant."

"All right," Derek said. "Then we will wait until tonight."

***

My father and Lucas left us temporarily to search for somewhere more comfortable, sheltered and away from creepy crawlies where we could pass the time.

When they returned from their exploration, they shared the same expression of awe.

"What is it?" my mother asked.

"We've located a dry cave that's fairly out-of-the-way, in one of the large mountains to the north," my father said. "But that's not all we found. We discovered where the IBSI's men are staying—and it's not in those little caravans we saw earlier. Those are just for toilets and refreshments."

"Well, where?" Derek asked tensely.

"They're staying in old Aviary city," my father replied, his eyes shining with wonder, as though his mind was still there. "Where Arron used to live." Where my father had been kept as a newborn…

"Much of it is still intact," Lucas said. "And it appears to have been completely abandoned by the Hawks. The hunters have taken up residence within the tree houses."

Wow. They were daring. They must have been pretty confident in their ability to fend off Hawks to do that. Then again, the Hawk population had weakened immensely since the war between Cruor and Aviary decades ago. Much of Aviary city was supposed to have been wrecked and abandoned in the struggle.

"So," my father concluded, "the good news is that Lucas and I know exactly where to head to eavesdrop later on. For now, let's all head to the cave."

It was a relief to arrive at the cave. Horatio smoked it out first, just to be sure there were no dangerous animals dwelling within. Hordes of shiny green beetles came scuttling out, along with the odd snake, clearing the way for us to step inside. He also kept his spell of shade over the area that he'd been holding up until now, for the sake of the vampires. Although it wouldn't be long until dark. The sun was already halfway along its descent in the sky. I was feeling a drop in temperature already.

Lucas and my father went off to fetch some wood— wood that was *not* derived from the peach-leaved trees— and we sparked a bonfire on the ledge outside the cave's entrance. I huddled close to it and scooped up a flame to hold in my palms. Orlando, whose knees still looked unsteady, dropped down next to me.

My mother handed us both an energy bar. Orlando

eyed the packaging, looking reluctant to eat anything. He was bracing his stomach with one hand, apparently experiencing a stomachache.

"Are you okay?" I asked, giving his forearm a gentle squeeze.

He nodded, wincing. "I guess."

"That was kind of crazy of you to volunteer," I said.

"Yep," he replied, stretching out his legs and leaning back against his elbows. "But sometimes, crazy works."

I couldn't disagree with that.

I tore open the wrapping of my bar and took a bite. I was still having trouble tasting food properly. This bar was banana and walnut—one of my favorites since I'd been a kid—and yet, as I chewed, I could hardly detect its flavor. It was like having a really bad cold; my tastebuds were muffled. But the bar was filling at least, and provided me with a dose of renewed energy.

The adults mostly retreated into the cave, except my father, Lucas, Aiden and Derek. They sat about ten feet in front of us, their legs hanging over the edge as they spoke in hushed tones and beheld the Jurassic land of Aviary at sunset.

I ate the last of my bar and scrunched the packaging into my pocket.

Orlando tossed me his. "Have mine too. I won't be eating for a while…"

I stuffed it into my backpack in case he or I wanted it later. Then I moved closer to him, allowing myself another long study of his face. I kept fearing that his paleness would return full force, but that touch of health still remained in his complexion.

"What do you see?" Orlando asked, his expectant eyes on mine.

"I see, uh…" *I see a brave man.*

"I still don't look as pale?"

I shook my head and realized that he *still* hadn't seen what he looked like. I moved into the cave and asked my mother if she had brought a travel mirror with her. She rummaged inside her backpack and found a small one. She handed it to me and I returned to Orlando, who was now leaning with his back against the wall of the mountain. I slumped down next to him, our hips an inch apart, and stretched out my feet until they almost touched the fire. I passed him the mirror. He studied himself in it with a frown. "Yeah, I see what you mean… I don't look like such a freak."

He set the mirror down and leaned his head back against the rock, his eyes half closed as he focused on the sunset. We were both lulled into a relaxed silence, the late evening chirping of birds and the low murmuring of our group surrounding us.

"You know," Orlando spoke in a low voice as the sun dipped out of sight, "I'm feeling something I haven't felt in a long time."

"What's that?" I asked him.

His eyes flitted to mine and lingered for a few seconds before returning to the sky. "Hope," he replied. "Real hope. The first time I felt it was just after you arrived in Chicago. When we stood on that rooftop and you persuaded me to talk to my sister about attempting escape with you…" He paused, swallowing. "You brought me hope, Grace, when I was in a very dark place. And, even if I never see my sister again, at least I can say she went out fighting. She always has been a fighter. It's just that city… it jaded her. But you brought the fire back in both of us."

I glanced uncomfortably at my feet. It didn't feel like I had done anything at all. I had just been desperate to escape that city, and I had needed the siblings to help me.

I wasn't sure how to respond, so I didn't.

"You know, I really think we are onto something with these trees," Orlando said, changing the subject. "If they can make a marked difference in me, imagine what they might do to you or for fully turned Bloodless?"

"Right," I said, staring into the crackling flames.

"But that's another thing you reminded me of," he went on thoughtfully. "Not to think too far ahead. To live in the now. We might have reason to hope we've made major progress today, but who knows what might happen tomorrow. It could all come crashing down around us as some kind of colossal misunderstanding. We could be back to square one. I could return to waking up every morning wondering whether I will live until the evening. I could die tomorrow. And so could you…" He wet his lower lip. His voice had risen with surprising passion over the course of his dialogue, but now it softened to a whisper, and I wasn't sure anymore whom he was really talking to—me or himself—as he said, "I realize it more and more. I *have* to live in the now."

I couldn't help but stare at him as firelight danced in his enlarged irises. My focus on him caused him to glance at me again, but this time, he didn't look away. He held my gaze steadily, shadows playing across his rugged face.

"You agree?" he breathed, his eyes searching mine.

I nodded, frowning slightly at the intensity of his question. Yes, of course I agreed one had to live in the now. Especially in circumstances such as these, otherwise—

I was in no way, shape or form prepared for what happened next.

Orlando's hand moved to my cheek. His fingers curved and entered my hair. His face descended until our noses touched and then our lips. He kissed me firmly, confidently. Like he'd kissed a hundred times before. When he drew away, it was as if he'd sucked the air from my lungs. My lips parting, I gaped at him.

Wh-What just happened?

CHAPTER 17: GRACE

I remained in a daze after Orlando drew away. His eyes stayed settled boldly on mine. My heart pummeled against my chest as it dawned on me that someone else might have noticed our kiss. I quickly looked around, but it seemed nobody had. My father, Lucas, Derek and Aiden still sat with their backs to us by the edge of the cave entrance, and Orlando and I were sitting in a corner, away from the direct view of those in the cave.

My gaze returned to Orlando. His heavy brows arched slightly in question. When I still didn't respond, it seemed to occur to him that he might've crossed a line.

"Grace, I'm sorry," he whispered. "I got carried away."

I gathered myself and rose to my feet. "I-I need to rest," was all I could manage, even as I winced. *The lamest response ever.* But in that moment, I just needed to get away from him. I needed some space for my brain to process what had just happened.

Orlando had kissed me.

He had claimed my first kiss.

I moved clumsily inside the cave and found a corner to sink into by myself. My mother noticed me and moved to approach but I shook my head. "You can stay over there," I told her, trying to sound normal. "I'm going to try and get some sleep."

"Good idea, honey," she replied, before resuming her seat next to Rose and Vivienne.

I curled up in one corner, turning my back on everyone and facing the jagged wall. My eyes remained wide open, though my vision glazed over. I realized that my hands were shaking slightly—I prayed only from the encounter with Orlando, and not because I was about to descend into another fit—and my breathing came fast and uneven.

I still wasn't sure how I felt about that kiss. Heck, I wasn't sure how I felt about Orlando. Despite all that we had been through together, he was still basically a stranger to me. As I was to him.

But maybe Orlando really hadn't meant much by it. Maybe he had simply been high on emotions after the events of the day, and when he'd started talking about living in the moment, he had just been tempted to do something crazy. Maybe I was reading too much into it. Maybe he didn't see a kiss as any big deal.

As much as I tried to tell myself that I shouldn't see it as a big deal either, it was. For me, a kiss *was* a big deal. A huge deal. It changed everything about Orlando's and my dynamic. My stomach clenched uncomfortably, and I felt a heavy dread at the thought of facing him again when I left the cave. *God, things are going to be so awkward between us now.*

I tried to shake myself to my senses. I had far greater things to worry about now than Orlando. *Like not turning into a vampire-zombie.* I figured I should close my eyes and try to forget about what had just happened.

Try to get some rest. And when it came time to leave, I should act like nothing happened. I didn't possess the emotional fortitude to get weighed down by this now.

I clamped my eyes tightly shut and tried to think of everything but Orlando. In my effort, my thoughts wandered to Lawrence. My mouth felt dry as I remembered the last evening we'd spent together in that old abandoned hotel in Scotland. How I had lain in his arms throughout the night... I couldn't help but feel that my first kiss should've taken place then, instead of tonight. And perhaps it would have, as the early morning hours drew in. Perhaps we would have found ourselves awake at the same time. Perhaps we would have caught each other's eye, and found our lips drawn together. But then Lawrence had descended into a fit, and soon after that he had slipped through my fingers. I hadn't even gotten the chance to say goodbye. And now he was lost to me.

I tossed and turned for hours, until my father announced that the hunters had packed up for the night. It felt very late by now; the IBSI must have had them working long days.

I dared to sit up and look toward the entrance, where my father stood addressing everyone. Beside him were Derek, Lucas and Aiden, while Orlando appeared to still be outside the cave. Maybe he was regretting kissing me.

"Lucas and I have already figured out where they keep the machinery after work—they park them up in that huge clearing we saw earlier," my father said. "So we can make our way there now. Though this is a job that has to be done extremely quietly so as to not alert anybody, and Horatio is the best person to do it... Magic is obviously quieter than any effort the rest of us would make to damage the equipment."

Everybody wanted to come in any case, so we all gathered together. I held my mother's hand and lowered my eyes firmly to the ground to avoid glimpsing Orlando joining the group.

Horatio transported us to the clearing we had come upon minutes after arriving in Aviary. It was an eerie sight to behold in the dark, this graveyard of trees. The lack of moonlight in the overcast sky made the shadows of machinery look like hulking monsters.

My eyes were drawn to the caravans, scattered near

each other in the center of the clearing. The blinds were drawn tightly shut in the windows, except for one of them, which emanated a warm orange light.

"Seems like someone's on night duty," I whispered, tugging on my father's arm and pointing toward the glowing caravan.

"Hence, we have to be stealthy," my father replied.

Our group sidled around the clearing, closer to where the machines started. Then Horatio left us and began moving among the vehicles. I wasn't sure exactly what he was doing as he circled each one and sometimes disappeared into them—but he was being utterly silent about it. Maybe he was putting some kind of irreversible freezing charm on the joints and other parts he figured were crucial.

We watched as he worked his way systematically through the vehicles until he reached the final row. Then our attention was drawn to the illuminated caravan, whose front door had just swung open. A tall, slim man stepped out, wearing pants and a vest. He was talking loudly into a phone. It took me but a few seconds to realize who it was; I should recognize his gravelly voice anywhere by now.

Atticus Conway.

Chapter 18: Grace

"Yes, I know it's late." Atticus spoke into the phone as he lit up a cigarette and pressed it to his lips. "But I only just arrived and I need you to give me a briefing… Mm. Mm. Yes, but we have already deduced the tree count isn't large. What is the estimate?"

"To hell with staying undercover," my father hissed behind me.

Before any of us could do or say anything, my father had shot away from our group and went hurtling toward Atticus. He moved so swiftly that Atticus didn't even realize he was upon him until it was too late. The phone and cigarette slipped from his grip as my father's hand closed around his mouth. My father wrestled him to the ground, stifling his grunts by pressing his face into the damp soil. Lucas and Horatio rushed over to help, Lucas disarmed Atticus while Horatio froze and silenced him with his powers.

Then the jinni levitated Atticus in the air and brought him floating back to us while my father and Lucas searched the caravan. Apparently finding it empty, they returned in a matter of seconds. We all gathered around the floating Atticus, whose face was a picture of fury.

"Let's get away from this clearing. Up to the trees," my father whispered.

Horatio transported us up to the treetops. He floated Atticus with his back against a thick trunk, facing forward.

"He needs to be able to speak," my grandfather said to Horatio. The jinni removed his charm. Atticus gasped for breath, his posture still rigid.

My father approached within a foot from Atticus and glowered at him. "What are you people doing here?" he demanded.

Atticus merely glared daggers at my father.

My father's hand closed around Atticus's throat. "What is the Bloodless antidote you are trying to keep hidden?" He pressed down against Atticus' Adam's apple.

The hunter kept his lips tightly sealed. Strangely, he didn't look even the slightest bit afraid.

"You'll kill me before you ever get me to talk," Atticus said coarsely, and somehow, I actually did believe him. Atticus didn't strike me as the type of man you could bargain with, or get through to, no matter how much you threatened him. His eyes glinted steely, uncompromising.

"We'll see about that," my father murmured. He turned to Horatio. "We should go further away still. But first we need to search him for a tracker. Silence him again in the meantime."

Horatio stole Atticus's voice again while laying the hunter flat on the ground. My father and grandfather searched him thoroughly, confiscating any weapons from his pockets and secret compartments in his clothing. They didn't spot a tracker in their efforts, though there was always the possibility that Atticus had one inserted internally for security. That would be too intrusive of an undertaking to take on now—and besides, even if his IBSI colleagues did come after him, with Horatio's help it shouldn't be too difficult to repel them.

The jinni returned us to the cave. They positioned Atticus at the cave's furthest wall before Horatio returned his voice. The jinni also lifted his freezing charm, allowing him to hold his own weight. My father resumed his interrogation. Atticus refused to utter a word. In spite of the threats, even in spite of a knife being held to his throat, he wouldn't reveal anything.

"Even if you kill me," Atticus informed us, "you will have accomplished nothing. Rest assured I've made certain of that."

I supposed by that he meant he had people who were second and third and fourth in command who could step up at a moment's notice.

My father backed away from Atticus and marched outside of the cave. We followed him.

"He's not responding to threats," he whispered to my

grandfather. "So the only way to see if he really is bluffing that he won't reveal anything is to start inflicting physical damage to him."

As vile of a person that Atticus was, my father still looked conflicted over the idea. Torture was a method that the IBSI readily used to pry information from people, but it was something that we in The Shade had always tried to avoid at all costs, even with our greatest enemies. We didn't want to stoop to the level of the IBSI, but it seemed that in this case, we would have no choice.

"Wait." I spoke up abruptly, finding my voice. "I-I want to speak to him first."

Everyone followed me as I returned to the cave and approached Atticus. I was keenly aware of the irony of the situation, of how our roles had reversed. The last time I'd come face-to-face with Atticus, he had been the one calling the shots and interrogating me.

I gritted my teeth and glared at the man. "What did you do to Lawrence?"

He barely even deigned to look at me as I arrived before him. His focus fixed firmly on the ceiling of the cave.

Anger boiled within me. I dropped my voice to a quieter, more menacing tone. "And what did you do to Georgina?"

At this, his mask broke. A flash of surprise crossed his face, and a definite disturbance.

"I know you killed her," I went on. "Her death was no accident. You had her assassinated." Of course, I didn't have solid evidence of this, but that didn't matter now. My only objective was to shake him. "I wonder what the world would think of the IBSI, if they really knew the truth about who runs it…"

He regained composure and refocused his eyes on the ceiling, determined even now not to waver.

Still, I pushed on regardless. "And I wonder even more how they would react if they knew that the IBSI was sitting on a cure for the Bloodless, and deliberately suppressing it. You people might control the media, but the truth always slips out in the end. *Always…* So I suggest you start talking, and we might agree to make this a little less painful for you."

As his eyelids flickered, in spite of his efforts to

maintain a poker face, I could see that my words had shaken him. We had discovered more than he thought.

But after a whole minute, he still hadn't spoken. I sank back in disappointment. It seemed that he really would rather die than give us the satisfaction of drawing a single answer from his lips. All this meant was that we were going to have to resort to torture…

Releasing an exasperated sigh, I stepped back, allowing my father to step forward. He was holding a knife in one hand, a gun in the other. The way my father's hands shook, I actually did believe that he was angry and desperate enough right now to murder the man. Desperation could drive even the most levelheaded of people to violence. *Atticus should know.*

My father began by grabbing Atticus' palm. I flinched as he sliced a gash across it, drawing blood. The first assertion that he meant business. "You know, Mr. Conway," my father said, "I have a lot to resent you for." He grabbed his second palm and etched another cut. I was flinching more than Atticus. Atticus' face had become stony again. "For the way you treated my daughter. For the way you've treated the rest of our

League. For the way you've cheated the entire world with your lies. It would be my honor and pleasure to end your life right now."

My father made a third cut into Atticus, at the base of his throat. Deep enough to draw a stream of blood, but not deep enough to damage a vital artery. I could no longer watch at this point.

I hated witnessing my father doing this. This wasn't like him. This wasn't like any of us.

"I'll give you twenty seconds to reconsider." My father's gun clicked. "Twenty seconds before this bullet will lodge in your brain."

"We will find out the details about the antidote, Atticus," my grandfather Derek implored. "Whether or not you speak, we will uncover it. In fact, we have our witches experimenting with the trees you have been felling as we speak. It might as well be—"

A screech pierced the night. It had emanated from outside of the cave.

We whirled to glimpse... mutants—five giant mutants, larger than I'd ever seen—landing with a heavy thump on the cliffside. Lithe men in black rode atop the beasts. I could only assume they had located us via a tracker installed beneath Atticus's skin, something we had already suspected he might have.

The mutants breathed out fire, which came rolling toward us at the back of the cave. The jinni manifested torrents of water to extinguish the blaze before it could reach us. The mutants continued to encroach. Horatio moved forward and billowed fire of his own, causing them to stall and stagger. As Horatio narrowed his eyes in focus, on the verge of creating a more deadly blast this time, the light from the flames flickered across the face of the hunter who rode the leading mutant.

An all too familiar face. A brown-eyed face.

Lawrence.

CHAPTER 19: GRACE

A hundred questions blasted through my brain as I caught sight of Lawrence's face. My mind felt blown to smithereens. But more than anything, urgency gripped me. Before Horatio could unleash another curse, I bellowed, "Wait, Horatio! Don't!"

My abrupt plea came as so unexpected to everyone that they became momentarily distracted from guarding Atticus. The hunter, sensing his opportunity, shot toward the mutants with such speed that none of our reflexes were fast enough. Within a split second, the mutant Lawrence sat upon had grabbed Atticus by the torso and with supernatural speed, the mutants immediately withdrew from the cave, as if they had been sucked out by an almighty vacuum.

My father, cursing, was on the verge of taking to the sky with Lucas and Horatio, but I caught hold of his hand before he could take off.

"Lawrence!" I panted. "One of those men was Lawrence!"

Everybody stared at me in disbelief.

"Grace, are you sure?" my mother breathed.

"Yes, I'm sure!" Lawrence had been on my mind so much since he'd left our island—probably more than was healthy—there was no way I had mistaken someone else for him. I could've sworn that he'd even met my eyes for just a second, but I hadn't detected even the slightest spark of recognition. His eyes had swept over me, as they had swept over all of us, in a steely gaze that reminded me uncannily of his father. Then he had swiped Atticus and fled.

But what on earth was Lawrence doing here? The last time I'd seen him on the television, he had looked so lost, so faded. A completely different person than the fiercely focused man I'd witnessed just now riding atop that mutant.

And why didn't he recognize me? He must have had his memory wiped again. It cut me to the core to think that all the time we'd spent together in The Shade would be forgotten to him.

My father shrugged me off. "I can't let Atticus get away!"

Still, I held onto him. "Atticus is useless for information," I reminded him urgently. "Absolutely useless! You saw it in his eyes. He would've died rather than give up his secrets. The only thing you'll gain by bringing him back is becoming his murderer."

"Then Lawrence," my father said. "If you truly think that was him, he must know something. I doubt he's as strong-willed as his father."

As much as I was desperate for a cure, I didn't know that I could stand to see my father torturing Lawrence the way he had Atticus. Even if Lawrence didn't remember me... I remembered him. Hot tears prickled the corners of my eyes. *Damn, I remember him.*

My father exhaled in aggravation as the mutants

disappeared into the trees. He began pacing up and down. "Well," he seethed, "we've done one thing for sure: blown our cover. Now they know that members of The Shadow League are here, and they know we know there's something special about the trees, and now..."

Now I couldn't help but wonder if it had been Lawrence on the other end of the phone Atticus had been holding when we'd first spotted him. Based on the snippet of conversation we'd heard, it sounded like it was Lawrence managing this whole Aviary operation, the way Atticus had asked him for a briefing. *Could he really be?* Horror filled me at the thought that Lawrence could be just as evil as his father. Maybe forgetting who he was before had been a good thing, and not something we should have ever tried to counteract...

"Lucas, I think we're going to have to resort to your idea."

My consciousness surfaced back to the present at my father's words.

My grandfather Derek locked eyes with his brother Lucas. "Are you up for returning to The Shade and gathering an army?" Derek asked. "Only one of us needs to go, but it has to be someone who can travel fast, which means either Ben, Horatio or you. But it would be wiser to keep Horatio here with us for protection."

"You're going to launch a full-on attack?" I choked.

"Grace," my father said, clutching my forearm. "We've got to stop them destroying these trees as soon as superhumanly possible. For all we know, Atticus could already be scheming to bomb this whole place and eradicate these trees within the next few hours. You heard him mention 'the tree count isn't large' on the phone, didn't you? What else could he be referring to but the poisonous trees? We've no choice but to rid Aviary of these hunters... and wreck as few trees as possible in the process."

"What about Atticus' laptop?" I stammered. I was hardly thinking straight. I just wanted to divert our attention to anything other than all-out war. "If he's here now, he might've brought it with him, with those files."

"I can guarantee you that anything he might have had on his laptop will be wiped the second he gets the chance," Lucas said, shaking his head. "And by the way, we checked the caravan. There was no laptop there. If he'd brought it with him, it should have been there, since he mentioned on the phone that he'd only just arrived in Aviary." Lucas' voice trailed off as his eyes trained on the distance, where the mutants had dipped out of view. "It looks like they are headed toward Aviary city now."

"We have to act quickly," my grandfather said. "Lucas"—he nodded grimly to his brother—"go. You know what to do."

Lucas nodded back, then sped away in the direction of the portal.

More bloodshed, I thought weakly. I had been hoping against hope that all this would not end in more bloodshed. But with the IBSI involved, how could I really expect anything different?

Chapter 20: Grace

At least the machinery had been meddled with, which would make it difficult for the IBSI to transport any explosives to get them where they needed them—assuming they did hold explosives here to begin with.

In spite of our hideout having been discovered, Horatio suggested we stay in the same cave and wait for Lucas, to avoid delays in him and our new recruits finding us. We shouldn't be waiting long anyway, given Lucas' supernatural speed.

But then my grandma Sofia countered, "Hopefully the IBSI doesn't have any witches hanging around nearby who might close the portal in the meantime. That would delay things for us a lot."

"That's a good point," Derek replied. "Maybe we should set up closer to the gate then, to keep an eye on it. Horatio?"

"Hm," Horatio said, stroking his jaw. "Yes. That might be a better idea. Then we'll have to stay alert for the others returning through it, so we don't miss each other."

Horatio transported us away from the cave and landed us in the treetops, almost directly above the portal. We tried to settle down and make ourselves somewhat comfortable as we waited, but I could hardly sit still for a moment.

Only a couple of hours ago, it had been Orlando occupying my mind, and I'd found it almost impossible to pry my thoughts from his kiss. Now, all that was practically forgotten. I was barely even aware of his presence a few feet away from me on the branch. Everyone surrounding me in the tree became invisible to me as those few seconds of my reunion with Lawrence played over and over in my mind like a broken record.

As lost as Lawrence seemed to me, I couldn't shake the doubt that he might not be like his father. That the Lawrence I had spent time with in The Shade had been genuine. That he was not inherently evil, and if I could somehow get him to realize the harm the IBSI had perpetrated, the real truth about the organization and his father's almost definite murder of his mother, I might get him to see the light, no matter how vigorously his mind had been programmed.

But if I was going to attempt this at all, I needed to find him before Lucas returned with an army… before the dragons arrived. I knew the chaos that would ensue. I would have no control over who got killed. Lawrence could easily be among the casualties.

"Are you okay?" A husky whisper came from my right. Orlando.

I focused my gaze on him. It was the first time I had looked him in the eye since he'd kissed me. I nodded slowly, even though the truth couldn't be further.

He inched closer to me, looking genuinely apologetic. "Hey, I'm sorry, okay?" he breathed. "I took things too far. Way too far. I just thought for a moment… you were thinking the same thing and, hell, it's been so damn long since I kissed a girl. And I… I've never kissed a girl quite like you."

He glanced away, sealing his lips.

Now was not the time for Orlando to be talking to me about this. I was too overwhelmed with anxiety to focus on his words.

"It's okay, Orlando," I murmured. I cast my attention firmly away from him—to Horatio, who sat on the other end of the branch. The jinni's head was panned downward as he kept a close eye on the portal. Orlando took the hint and backed away, giving me some much-appreciated space.

I realized as I watched the jinni how dry my throat was feeling. I reached into my backpack and grabbed my water. I downed the whole bottle in a matter of minutes, but still, the uncomfortable scratchy feeling at the back of my mouth didn't subside. Not in the least.

I looked toward my mother and was about to ask her for some more water when my throat closed up. I began to choke.

Oh, no. No. Not again.

I began hacking as though I was trying to cough my organs out, and then came blood. Drops of blood, raining from my mouth onto my knees and open palms. As I continued coughing, I was expelling far too much blood for comfort.

Oh, God. I'm getting worse.

Orlando and my parents, who were nearest to me, hurried to stabilize me on the branch so that I would not slip as tremors claimed my body again. They lasted longer than ever before, each one more powerful, more violent. My skull banged against the branch. My teeth chattered. My extremities felt like ice cubes and tingled like they were being punctured by needles.

When the fit subsided, and I attempted to sit up slowly—Orlando and my parents still gripping hold of me to keep me steady—I already knew that it had not left me the same person.

I knew instantly from the look on Orlando's and my parents' faces.

"What is it?" I demanded in a panic.

Their eyes were roaming the length of me.

I glanced down at my hands and realized just how

much paler they looked all of a sudden. Paler and more… veiny. I twisted my hands so that my wrists were visible. Blue veins jutted out so far my arms had become practically unrecognizable. *These are not my wrists.*

"Hand me a mirror," I stammered to my mother, even as I feared I would regret it.

"Grace," she gasped.

"Please! Just hand one to me," I begged.

She dipped into her backpack and rummaged. "Oh, I handed my travel mirror to you earlier, darling," she said. "You never gave it back."

Dammit. I must've left it back at the cave.

My aunt Rose's concerned face appeared within my view. Her expression was a mirror of the others'.

"I have a mirror, but—" Rose said.

"Then let me see myself!" I cried, too loudly.

Rose searched her bag and pulled out a foldable mirror. Trembling, I pried it open and stared at myself. As I had feared, the tone of my face had changed drastically, just like the rest of my body. And it was as if my skin had thinned. Blue veins were also visible where there had been no trace of them before, especially near my temples.

I clapped the mirror shut and flung it back to my aunt, terrified of my reflection. My father's hand closed around my shoulder. "Grace, it's time to take you back to The Shade. We are just asking for trouble dragging you around with—"

"No," I insisted. "That won't solve *anything*! I would turn there just as I am now! No," I repeated, in a quieter though no less desperate tone, "That's not what I need… I need to get through to Lawrence."

Chapter 21: Lawrence

I was feeling beyond confused as I carried my father back with me and my colleagues to Aviary city.

What had just happened?

Who were those people who had taken my father hostage?

One moment I had been on the phone to my father, filling him in on the progress we'd made and the remaining estimated tree count, and the next I'd heard him grunt, followed by the thump of the phone hitting the ground.

I'd set out with an emergency search party

immediately, though it wasn't difficult to find him. As was mandatory for all IBSI members recruited to work on the new construction site in Aviary, as soon as we arrived in this land, we had to hook ourselves up to a central tracing system based in one of the technology caravan units in the center of the main clearing ground. For such a large project as this, it was mandatory that I had the means to know where everyone was, to manage our resources and ensure that everybody was working together as efficiently as possible… In all honesty, I was surprised that my father had given me such a prominent role so soon after my successful drug trial. I found the attention he was showing me now rather difficult to get used to, though it certainly was not unwelcome. I had been all but estranged from him while growing up. After my mother's accident, I'd rarely seen him. It was understandable, of course. He had arguably the most demanding job in the world.

Now, he thought I was up to managing the IBSI's activities in Aviary. He assured me that I was a fast learner and would easily fill in the gaps in my knowledge while on the job.

So far, he was right—it hadn't been difficult to slip into this role, even if I did find myself asking several times a day what exactly I was doing in this position of authority.

We arrived at our temporary base among the treetops in old Aviary city. We had cleared away the medieval treehouses that been perched among the branches and replaced them with glass box-like constructions with interconnecting walkways. There were over a hundred rooms in this sprawling architecture, and that was with some workers sharing a room. My father and I parted ways with the other men, and landed directly on top of one of the walkways with the mutant. The creature set my father down before I slid off myself. I gave the mutant a nod, indicating that I had finished with him for now and he ought to rejoin the others.

Riding these... *things* was a skill I had not forgotten. There were many others that I remembered, too. It was only a period of a couple of months that had been completely erased from my memory during the drug procedure—and my father said that I was lucky, since two months was a very short period. Much less than expected. He said that, before I'd gone in, they had predicted I might even lose up to a year of my life.

My last memory was my graduation day from Creston Academy, an elite training center for future IBSI members. I recalled all the training that led up to my graduation, and then on the actual day, I remembered the elation I'd felt as I'd been getting ready to attend the ceremony. More than anything, I recalled imagining my father being present among the crowds. I wished that I could remember him actually being there, but my memory cut short after that and returned only after waking up from the drug-induced coma to be informed that my transformation was complete. I didn't remember the day I'd discovered that my father was looking for volunteers for a drug trial, or his initial reluctance to allow me to volunteer, or his eventual agreement when I had insisted. I'd had to rely on my father to fill in these gaps for me.

We climbed through a glass trap door in the roof of the walkway and emerged in a communal kitchen.

"Who were those people?" I asked. "They looked like supernaturals."

"You know," my father said, looking irritated as he leapt up and yanked the trap door shut above us, "I've told you about them before. They're rogue agents, from that little island in the Pacific. They've been seething ever since they got dropped from their official roles. Blaming us for their incompetence, they take every opportunity to sabotage our work. They were the instigators of the massacres that took place in The Woodlands and The Trunchlands—didn't I mention that?"

"Yeah," I murmured. "You did."

He retrieved a first aid kit from one of the shelves. I watched him sterilize and bandage his wounds.

"Why do they bother?" I couldn't help but ask. "Seems a stupid amount of effort to follow us around."

He turned his back on me and reached into his right pocket, drawing out a pack of supplements. "As I said, they are bitter," he said, popping a round green pill into his mouth—the same pill I took mornings and evenings, along with a plethora of others. He heaved a sigh. "Basically, they've somehow gotten it into their heads that we shouldn't be felling these poisonous trees. They don't understand that we need to create space here. The base that we'll build in the coming months will prove to be invaluable to our defense strategy, as we've discussed."

I nodded, reaching for my own bottle of water. Although I had not gripped it hard, the plastic dented beneath my touch, and I had to remind myself to ease up a little. I still was not close to being used to this new body I'd woken up in. My father told me that certain aspects of my strength had the potential to rival even that of a vampire when I was on the right cocktail of supplements. My father was to undergo the same procedure as myself soon, as were a dozen other IBSI members. The rigid regimen of supplements he was taking every day was preparation for this.

As I swallowed down my water, I thought back to something else in that cave that I'd found odd—that young woman who'd yelled out for the magic-wielder to stop.

But my father didn't appear to be in any mood to continue discussing the matter.

"So what's going to happen now?" I asked him, frowning. He leaned against the counter and rubbed his temples. "Are we just going to allow them to roam freely around Aviary and continue causing us trouble? What if there are more of them than those we found in that cave? And what if there are more *dangerous* League members, like dragons?"

My father nodded, lowering his hands again to his sides and holding my gaze. "You're right, Lawrence. We can't have them meddling, and we *definitely* can't have a repeat of the slaughter they carried out in The Woodlands or The Trunchlands. And we won't have either..." My father tightened his belt around his waist before concluding, "I'll keep you informed."

I raised my brows. "Well, what are you planning to do?"

"Leave it to me," he said shortly. "You just get some sleep, it's been a long day. And stay inside. You won't want to be stepping out for a while... You'll soon realize why."

I frowned as my father left the room. *What is he planning?*

I helped myself to a protein shake. Gulping it down, I gazed out through the glass into the dark treetops surrounding us. They swayed to a breeze I couldn't hear, the occasional shaft of moonlight spilling down to illuminate their broad, tapered leaves.

There were times when I felt that the things my father told me were only the tip of the iceberg. Times I wished that his explanations were more detailed… but this was the way he was. A busy man who wasn't accustomed to stopping to explain. I was used to that. I'd had my whole childhood to get used to that.

I wasn't wondering long what he had planned, however. After finishing my shake and returning along the walkways to my room, I glanced out of the window again and noticed a thick smoke with a greenish tinge had descended outside the glass. So thick that I could hardly see through it.

I dropped to my mattress, staring at the mist billowing around the glass construction. I knew what this was.

I just hadn't been expecting us to use it so soon.

CHAPTER 22: LUCAS

I traveled back to The Shade with speed and focus. Hardly any time was wasted in getting lost over the ocean. Over the past couple of decades, I had traveled the waters surrounding The Shade and America so much that I knew the landmarks like the back of my hand… *well, almost.*

Since I didn't have automatic permission to enter The Shade—only witches and a select number of jinni had that—I was forced to yell my throat hoarse for someone to come and let me in.

It was Corrine who arrived. Perfunctory at first on

eyeing me, as always, she performed a routine check to verify that I was not an imposter before asking, "What is going on, Lucas?"

"I need to gather an army," I replied grimly, soaring with her through the redwoods and touching down on the forest ground.

I proceeded to explain to her what had happened since Ibrahim left our company—which wasn't long ago. Corrine informed me that it'd taken the witches and jinn a while to respond to my yelling because they'd all been so wrapped up with the tree specimens Ibrahim had brought back.

"So far, we haven't made any breakthroughs," she confirmed. "But we haven't had much time."

"Okay," I said. "Well, I'm going to need to borrow a few witches to help us chase the hunters out of Aviary. I will also need dragons, wolves, more jinn, and anybody else who is able and capable."

Corrine agreed to gather the witches and jinn, while I headed off to gather the rest of the League. I informed them that if they were willing to embark on this mission, they needed to gather by the Port within half an hour. I deliberately left out my son, Jeramiah, however. Derek rebuked me for it on occasion, but I tried to keep him out of the League's activities as much as I possibly could. It had taken me decades to be reunited with that boy, and I wasn't as tolerant about watching him ride into danger as the other parents of the island were... even though he was a fully grown adult.

Yuri, Kiev and a couple of the dragons helped me gather weapons and explosives from the Armory, and then all we could do was wait for the rest to arrive before the deadline.

I was about as good at waiting as I was at cooking—always had been that way. I found myself pacing up and down, leaving the clearing and heading to the beach to try to distract myself by watching the waves.

I mulled over question after question relating to the IBSI and the so-called antidote. I hoped that, for Grace's sake, we weren't barking up the wrong tree... so to speak.

I glanced back again at the Port after a couple of minutes and was pleased to see more League members had gathered by now. I was about to return to speak to the newest arrivals when a feminine voice called behind me.

"Monsieur Novak."

I turned on my heel to find myself gazing down into a pair of pretty hazel eyes. A delicate face, framed by locks of blonde-streaked brown hair. It took a few seconds for it to register in my brain that this was Marion, the young woman I had saved along with her baby back in The Trunchlands. She looked so different now than when I had last seen her. She had a healthy glow to her cheeks. Her hair was clean and combed in soft curls. The witches must have also managed to make her put on a few pounds, because her previously emaciated form had become distinctly curved beneath a light yellow dress.

The vision of her caused me to temporarily abandon my resolve to greet the new recruits, and I found myself standing at her and staring. "Uh, hello," spilled from my lips. "I mean, *bonjour.*"

She smiled broadly. A smile that emphasized the delicate apples of her cheeks… and even a small splash of freckles across her nose, now that her skin was bright and clean.

"How is your, uh, *enfant?*" I asked. *Damn. My French ought to be better than this.*

"Avril is happy," she said, her eyes lighting up. "She… sleeping in hospital. With nurse."

"Oh, good," I said. My chest tensed as she continued gazing up at me.

"Monsieur Novak—" she began again.

"Please, call me Lucas."

She smiled coyly. "Lucas." My name coming from her lips sent an odd tingle down my spine. "I thank you again for helping me and my baby."

"Oh, that's… really no problem."

"Hey, Lucas!" Kiev yelled. "Everyone's arrived."

As selfish as it was, I realized a small part of me had actually been hoping that some League members would arrive a little later. I returned my eyes to Marion's bright face. I let out a breath. "I'm sorry, Marion. I need to go."

"Where do you go?" she asked curiously.

"To battle."

She raised her brows. "Battle?"

"You know… War. Fight." I balled up my fists and

held them up in a stupid gesture of combat.

Understanding dawned on her face. "Oh. You are… warrior."

I couldn't stop a small smile from cracking my lips. "Well, yes… I guess you could say I'm a warrior—"

"Lucas!" Kiev roared. "What the hell are you doing? Get over here!"

"I have to go," I told Marion apologetically.

"*Mais oui!* Of course! Be careful… Lucas."

That shiver again.

I lowered my head slightly in a bow. Meeting her wide eyes once more, I turned on my heels. But before I could take a step, her hand reached out and closed around mine. The next thing I knew, I was being tugged downward, and her heart-shaped lips were pressing against my right cheek. Her kiss was both soft and firm, and infused with passion.

Then she pulled away just as suddenly, her cheeks flushed… As I knew mine were.

"*Adieu,*" she whispered breathlessly.

"*A-Adieu,*" I managed.

I finally tore myself away from Marion and sped back

toward Kiev, who had by now descended from the jetty and appeared to be on his way to physically grab me. Though my right cheek remained tingling far longer than it should have.

Chapter 23: Ben

I stared down at my daughter's pale, sweaty face as she begged me, "Please. I need to speak to Lawrence."

I could hardly bear to glance at River. Neither of us had ever experienced as much pain as this before—to witness our daughter turning before our very eyes while we watched helplessly.

But we had to hold it together. Neither of us could crack in front of Grace. I swallowed hard and set my focus firmly on my daughter.

"All right," I said. "I'll go find him."

"Thank you," she breathed, settling her head back

down against the branch.

I was doubtful that a talk with Lawrence would gain us anything, even if I did manage to arrange it. He appeared to have been completely reprogrammed—an ally of the IBSI, no longer the confused boy who'd woken up in The Shade and developed a friendship with my daughter. But I couldn't deny Grace's request. Not at a time like this. After kissing her forehead and exchanging a fleeting glance with my wife, I left the group on the branch, even as I prayed that Grace would not undergo another fit while I was gone.

I hurried toward Aviary city. Along the route, I couldn't help but notice the peachy, poisonous trees growing sparser and sparser, until I couldn't spot a single one and they gave way to another species of tree entirely.

As I neared the city that had once been my prison, it looked nothing like it used to. I had been too young to remember anything when I'd been brought here, of course—I'd been only an infant—but I'd had visions of it since then in my later years. Gone were the tree houses carved of wood, straw and leaves, and gone were the rope bridges connecting one trunk to the other. In their place was an intricate network of metal and glass boxes, linked together by cylindrical walkways. An odd green mist hung in the air, obscuring parts of the IBSI's constructions entirely. It didn't look like a natural gas that might occur in Aviary. It looked to me more like some sort of insect or animal repellent, probably to keep the hunters undisturbed in the dark hours. It appeared to be spreading quickly, moving in my direction. I breathed in, sensing no strong odor to it.

I sank into the nearest box and found myself in a dark bedroom. Gray venetian blinds were drawn against the window. A bunkbed lined one of the walls, where two men slept. I leaned over the hunter on the bottom bunk to see if I recognized him—a man in his late twenties. I didn't recognize him, nor the man sleeping above him.

After our kidnapping of Atticus, I found it strange that any hunter would be sleeping. I would've thought that Atticus would have immediately sounded an alarm and put everyone on alert for an impending attack.

I moved through the walls to the next room and found yet another sleeping hunter. As I continued to travel from room to room through the spidery network, practically every one contained sleeping hunters. And those hunters I passed who were awake had been relaxing, playing cards with a roommate, or reading a book.

Something odd was going on.

But I couldn't allow my mind to wander too far off my goal. *Lawrence.* I'd promised my daughter I'd find him. As Atticus's son, I figured that he would be positioned in one of the more central rooms, where in theory he would be surrounded by more security. By the time I had worked my way toward what seemed to be the most central area, the atmosphere outside had become completely choked with smoke.

Finally, I came across Lawrence. Despite the transformation of his physique, I recognized his face instantly beneath dimmed lights. He was lying on his back on a mattress in a room he clearly had to himself. His eyes were closed, though he was breathing lightly. It was hard to tell whether or not he had fallen asleep yet.

I paused, considering what my next move should be. I was tempted to grab him from his bed and carry him away, but that would be more complicated than it sounded. He wasn't a fae like me, and he couldn't pass through solid walls. I had spotted a trap door above a kitchen nearby that appeared to be unlocked, but I would have to transport him there first. If he started yelling, it would attract attention.

I didn't know what the IBSI was playing at by not immediately gearing itself up for a fight, but I sensed in my gut that none of us should be causing a disturbance until our recruits arrived. He might be shocked to open his eyes to a strange girl in his room—I would be sure to keep out of sight—but less so than a strange man carrying him off in the middle of the night.

My eyes lingered on Lawrence a few seconds more. Then I left his room and emerged once again in the smoke. I raced back the way I came, toward the tree where I had left Grace and the others.

The smoke truly was spreading rapidly. It had now engulfed the area of old Aviary city and was drifting its way through the jungle.

Where was it coming from? There must have been hidden canisters somewhere that released the substance.

On arriving among the peachy-leaved trees, the smoke

hadn't reached them yet. The air was still clear and crisp.

I reached the tree where my family awaited. Grace was lying on her back, River beside her, holding our daughter's forehead. I searched my wife's face for indication of whether Grace had had another incident in my absence. "Grace is doing okay," River managed.

Grace sat bolt upright on spotting me through the gloom.

I took her frail hand in mine. "I found Lawrence, Grace. Come with me."

Her lips parted in relief. "Oh, thank God," she breathed.

"If you're heading back there with Grace, take Horatio with you," my father said, looking worried. "We can manage without him for a short while... Just don't be too long."

I nodded, gritting my teeth. "We won't."

Chapter 24: Derek

This was becoming torturous. Now we were waiting not only for my brother to return with recruits, but for my son, granddaughter and Horatio. Nobody uttered a word as we perched wide-eyed in the trees. I kept my eyes fixed on the portal on the ground, willing my brother to appear. I didn't think I had ever wished for his presence as much as I did now.

A chorus of cawing broke out above us. It sounded like the noise of large birds flying overhead, booming and sonorous.

Startled, Sofia moved closer to me and placed a hand

on my knee. She didn't say anything, but the gesture was reassuring. Sofia's touch always had a way of reassuring me, no matter the circumstances. I wrapped an arm around her and held her closer to me on the branch as we waited.

Twigs snapped beneath us. Leaves crunched. I heard the noise of an engine. Leaving Sofia's side, I quickly swung lower down the tree to gain a better view of the ground. A motorcycle thundered along the wide track that led to the portal. A trailer was strapped to it, its contents covered by a tarpaulin sheet. I was dismayed to see a vehicle working, though it was unreasonable to think that they had kept every single piece of machinery in the clearing for Horatio to tinker with.

The motorcycle's bright lights flashed in the darkness, and then it stopped about twelve feet in front of the portal. It was impossible to see who was riding it, though it appeared to be a man. He was wearing some kind of mask that obscured his head and face entirely.

He pulled back the tarpaulin and dipped down into the trailer, withdrawing a large cylinder. As he offloaded it, placed it upright and swiftly yanked down on a lever to its right, alarm bells were already ringing through my head.

A hissing sound burst from the cylinder, followed by streams of thick greenish vapor.

"We need to get out of here," I breathed, rushing back up to the branches where my family waited. "We need to move!" I urged. I had no idea what that green smoke was, but I knew it wasn't good news.

"Wha-What's happening?" Rose stammered.

"Where do we move?" Sofia asked, alarmed. "We need to keep an eye on the portal."

"Forget the portal for now," I shot back. "We have no—"

The hissing intensified to almost a scream. I swung back down to the lower branches in time to witness the cylinder shoot upward through the trees like a rocket. It imploded with a dull crack as it reached the roof of leaves, and the green gas that had been shooting out in streams spilled out into the area with such force, it surrounded us in a matter of seconds. I heard the motorcycle retreating.

"What in the world…" Sofia gasped next to me. I

clung to her, barely able to even make her out in this fog. It stung my eyes like it was toxic.

We have to get away from here. As I cast my eyes about, trying to figure out which direction appeared to have been affected by the strange gas the least, a heavy nausea set in. It felt like I had just run headfirst into a brick wall, or been walloped by an iron bar. One moment I was racking my brain for an escape route, and the next I could barely form a coherent thought. As if the smoke surrounding us wasn't thick enough, my vision began to cloud. I could hardly see even a foot in front of me. Sofia slipped from my grip. I struggled to hold on to her, even as my limbs felt like jelly.

Everything started happening in slow motion. Members of my family dropped from the tree like flies, unable to support their own weight. The smoke intensified… and then my eyes gradually closed.

In my last few seconds of consciousness, I cursed myself for not getting everyone down to the ground the moment that hunter had pulled out a cylinder. We might have not known what danger we'd meet with down there, but at least we wouldn't have had to contend with the fall…

But it was too late now.

Far too late.

Chapter 25: Grace

As I traveled with Horatio and my father, we soon encountered a strange greenish fog. Before I could draw in more than a breath, my father clamped a hand over my mouth and blocked my nostrils. "Horatio, put up some kind of vacuum around us, will you?" he addressed the jinni.

Horatio's nose curled as he eyed the smoke before he proceeded to create a bubble of clear air around us. My father removed his hand from my face, allowing me to breathe normally again.

"I passed through this smoke before," my father

explained, "and it doesn't seem to have any effect on fae, but Grace might respond to it differently."

"What is this?" I asked, gazing around.

"I assume it's some kind of strong pesticide the hunters are using to keep this place clear of dangerous predators. But... I'm not sure," he added, concerned.

My focus left the smoke and returned to Lawrence. My gut writhed. The thought of seeing him again, of standing face to face with him, was both exhilarating and terrifying. I knew it could be a completely wasted attempt—he might not be able to recall anything about me, and refuse to even hear me out... but I had to try.

"All right, we're close now," my father announced, our bubble passing through a particularly thick patch of smoke.

I could make out only the vague outline of square-shaped constructions among the treetops. We moved to the roof of a cylindrical walkway.

"You can take us inside, Horatio," he whispered.

The jinni made us invisible, removed the protective bubble, and then used his magic to transport us within the cylinder. Inside, all was deathly quiet. It was like being locked up in a soundproof box. A chemical smell filled my nostrils, some kind of mild detergent.

Our breathing seemed loud in the quiet. "Follow us, Horatio," my father said. He gripped me and pulled me forward, out of the walkway, through a small communal kitchen, and then down a hallway lined with doors leading to rooms on either side. When he finally stopped outside one of the doors, my skin was tingling.

"Now, Horatio," my father whispered in a voice barely louder than a breath. "You and I need to stay invisible. But you can remove your magic from Grace. Then transport all three of us to the other side of this door. We will stand by, and watch what happens… Grace." My father's mouth lowered to my ear. "We won't let anything happen to you, I promise."

I nodded, though strangely, that was the last thing on my mind. Given the fact that I had no idea what state Lawrence would be in, perhaps my safety around him was something I should've been concerned about.

Horatio proceeded to execute my father's instructions. The dimly lit hallway surrounding us disappeared and we found ourselves in a much darker room. Square and lit by a single dimmed lamp in one corner of the room, the room contained little more than a narrow desk, a chair, and a bed… A bed that held a young man. Lawrence.

My voice caught in my throat as I laid eyes on him, spread out across his mattress on his back, his face panned to the ceiling. He wore nightclothes—a white shirt that parted to reveal his toned upper chest, and loose black pants.

I looked behind me instinctively toward where I imagined my father and Horatio were standing, and gave them a final nod. It was more a gesture of resolve to myself than to them.

I moved cautiously across the slate-gray carpet toward the end of Lawrence's bed. My eyes felt wide as saucers as I looked him over. His eyes were closed, and all signs indicated that he had fallen asleep. He breathed evenly, his firm lips ever so slightly parted. Gulping, I made my way around the side of the bed until I was standing level with his head.

"Lawrence," I managed to whisper.

No response. Not even the slightest twitch of an eye.

He remained still, as if I hadn't spoken. "Lawrence," I repeated.

Still no response. I dared reach out a hand and place it over his forehead. Surely my coldness should be enough to wake anybody up.

Still, he remained in slumber.

I had wanted to avoid grabbing him and shaking him—that certainly wasn't the best way for him to wake up to a stranger in his room. But it seemed that I would have no choice. I planted both hands on his shoulders and shook him hard.

Still he didn't wake.

What the heck is going on? It's like he's dead.

"Horatio," I hissed. "I need some help."

The jinni manifested himself and grabbed Lawrence by the ankle. With his supernatural strength, he yanked him right off the bed and dangled him upside down in mid air.

Okay, I'd been hoping Horatio would have been a little more subtle than that... but it still didn't work.

I gaped at Lawrence's sleeping form as Horatio plonked him back down on the bed. I found myself reaching for his neck to verify his pulse, to confirm that the heave and sigh of his chest was not just some kind of illusion. Yes, he was alive.

Then why in heaven's name isn't he waking up?

Chapter 26: Lucas

My mind was still flitting embarrassingly often to Marion as we traveled to the portal in Bermuda. I supposed I had a thing for French girls.

But as we arrived and prepared to leap through the gate to Aviary, it was time to push her from my mind.

It had come as a surprise to all of us to find the portal unmanned. After what we'd done to Atticus, I would have thought hunters would be teeming everywhere by now.

But nope. It was quiet as a cemetery.

We gathered around the portal and piled through one

by one. This portal was wide enough for the dragons—led by Jeriad—to pass through in their beastly forms, which was convenient. We let them jump through first to clear the way, in case there was any opposition waiting for us on the other end. Then the rest of us—witches, jinn, vampires, werewolves and another fae, Kailyn—followed. Arwen, Brock and Heath, three of the League's newest recruits, had accompanied us, too.

I was the last to shoot through the abyss, and the second I arrived on the other side, I already knew something was wrong. Very wrong. The jungle was choked with thick green smoke, so thick that I could hardly see three feet in front of me. The sound of everyone coughing filled my ears. I breathed in cautiously, trying to detect if the smoke had any scent, but at least to my nose, it was odorless.

"What is this?" Jeriad rasped.

"We need to get away from this area!" I hissed, even as I tried to keep my voice down. We had no idea where hunters might be located. This could be some sort of trap for all I knew. We had to get to the cave where I'd left my brother and the others. I hoped they'd still be there.

"Shayla," I called to one of the witches who had been spared to come with us. "Safi," I addressed the nearest jinn I could make out through the smog. I pointed eastward, the approximate direction of the cave. "You need to start transporting us that way."

"Argh!" Yuri choked just behind me. I whirled and, to my horror, found him fallen on the ground. He was clutching his throat and wheezing uncontrollably. Claudia, a couple of feet next to him, stumbled and tripped beside him.

I cursed.

All around me, our people were collapsing.

As I turned to yell at Shayla and the jinn to hurry the hell up, I realized that Shayla had broken down coughing too. Dashing to her in a panic, I almost tripped over Kiev's form in the undergrowth. It seemed that the only supernaturals left unaffected were the fae and the jinn. Vampires, witches, werewolves, and heck, even the dragons had collapsed.

Dammit! What is this stuff? Fumes so strong they can debilitate even a dragon?

Whatever this smoke was, I prayed that it wasn't fatal. As the jinn hurried to gather everyone together so that we could be sure to not leave anyone behind, Kailyn's voice rang through the trees. "Oh, my God! Look!"

I swiveled and rushed toward her voice. She came into view about six feet away from me. She was crouched down on the ground, hovering over... my sister.

"Vivienne," I gasped, dropping to my knees and clutching her shoulders. She was sprawled out on the damp soil, eyes closed. Her lips were swollen and purple, her clothes ripped. On one side of her head was a protruding bump. *What in heavens...*

I scooped my sister up in my arms, relieved that she was still breathing at least.

But what was she doing all the way over here? They were supposed to be waiting for us in the cave.

"Where are the others?" I demanded aloud, as if expecting the jungle to throw me back an answer.

Then my eyes fell on another body, partly obscured by a bush. I hurried over and pushed the shrubbery aside to uncover Caleb. He was in no better state than Vivienne, bumps and bruises littering his body. It was like they had fallen… a long distance.

My head panned upward. More bodies hung above me, scattered awkwardly among the branches. Members of my family. All of them unconscious.

I didn't have time to ask more questions. Thank God we hadn't left here yet, and Kailyn had ventured a little further out in her search.

"Guys," I called to the jinn, fearful they might leave prematurely. "Wait! We've got more people over here!" I carried Vivienne to the rest of our unconscious army while Kailyn carried Caleb, before we returned to begin disentangling the others from the trees. I spotted Sofia next, balancing precariously on her midriff, her hands and feet dangling on either side of a thick branch. I gathered her to me and handed her to Kailyn, who zoomed her back to the jinn. Next, we helped Xavier, Aiden, River and her siblings, Orlando and Rose, who had alarmingly wound up in the coils of a monstrous red-scaled snake. She'd been lucky to get out of its grip without being squeezed to a pulp, or eaten—I assumed her bitter vampire blood had been the only thing stalling the snake from digging its fangs into her. I approached the snake from behind, gripped its head and squeezed its neck until it gave her up.

Now those still missing were Grace, Ben, Horatio and Derek. As much as we searched among the branches of all the neighboring trees, and then headed to the ground to do a thorough search of the undergrowth, we couldn't find them anywhere.

We couldn't stall any longer. We had to get the others away from here—to some fresh air.

But now I was in a quandary. If those who were supposed to be in the cave had migrated here, perhaps that meant something had happened there. Maybe they'd been forced to leave. In which case, it made no sense to return there now.

Exhaling sharply, I hissed, "Take them back through the portal to Bermuda. Find a safe spot and do whatever you can to revive them. If you fail then take them back to The Shade."

I hated the idea of everyone retreating so soon—of being outsmarted by the hunters so quickly—but there wasn't room for pride in this situation. I was just terrified for everyone's lives right now. I felt grateful that I had avoided alerting Jeramiah to this mission.

"And what will you do? Are you coming?" Safi called back. "And where is Horatio?"

It was probably a good thing that Horatio had insisted Aisha stay back from this mission, too, or she would be worried out of her mind for her husband.

I exchanged glances with Kailyn. It was clear from her expression that she would stay with me. "We need to stay and find the others," I replied to Safi.

She nodded before she and the other jinn transported the rest of our people through the gate.

I let out a shallow sigh of relief. At least we had gotten *them* out of here.

What a mess this is…

Now we had to scour this jungle for the missing four.

Kailyn and I soared further away from the portal. As we passed poison tree after poison tree, I suddenly noticed something I hadn't before. Something that had escaped my attention due to my brain being primarily focused on searching for the forms of my family among the branches.

The peachy-colored leaves. They looked different.

Previously smooth and bloated, they now looked shriveled and wrinkly, as though the fluid had been sucked out of them.

I gazed around to check that we hadn't just come across an anomaly, but we hadn't. Every leaf within sight had been altered.

"Oh, dear," Kailyn breathed. "Whatever this gas is, it seems to be serving a dual purpose…"

CHAPTER 27: GRACE

So this wasn't exactly how I'd imagined my reunion with Lawrence would go—standing tensely at the edge of the room while watching him being dangled up and down by Horatio like a sack of potatoes.

After the jinni had failed to wake him with that method, since Lawrence was still breathing and obviously not dead, I could only assume that his profound sleep had something to do with his recent transformation. Maybe this was normal. But we didn't have all night to figure it out.

I spotted a mini-cooler beneath a dressing table. I

AN HOUR OF NEED

stooped down to it and opened the door. It was filled with chilled glass bottles of water.

After all that shaking, would cold water have a chance of waking him? I gritted my teeth. *If I pour it over him the right way it should...*

I emptied the cooler of water with the help of my father, and together we hurriedly unscrewed all the lids and placed the bottles on the bedside table closest to Lawrence's head. I grabbed one of the sheets from his bed and folded it up so that it was just wide enough to fit over the lower portion of his face. Placing it firmly over his mouth and nose, I reached for the first bottle and tipped it onto the cloth.

I hated to resort to waterboarding, but this guy just wasn't waking up.

The water spilling down Lawrence's nostrils and blocking his airways finally made him stir. God only knew what spell he'd been under to make him sleep so deeply. As he coughed and spluttered, I quickly shot Horatio and my father a look, indicating that they make themselves invisible.

As they disappeared, Lawrence's hands moved to his

face. I managed to remove my hand just in time before his fingers curled around the wet sheet and threw it away from his face.

I staggered back as he sat bolt upright, his eyes wide and shining, his wet hair licking the sides of his face. The next thing I knew, he had jerked backward. He threw himself off the bed and whipped out a gun from a hidden pocket in the side of the mattress. Kneeling on the floor, he aimed it at me.

"Wait!" I hissed, holding up my hands. I was addressing Horatio and my father just as much as Lawrence. If they manifested now, this would all be over before we'd even started. It looked like it was going to be hard enough to get through to Lawrence on my own, let alone with two strange men in the room too.

"Who-Who are you?" Lawrence demanded. His familiar British voice took on a fierce tone I wasn't used to.

I knelt before him on the bed. "My name is Grace," I whispered urgently. "Grace Novak. You know me... Or knew me. I mean you no harm. Please. I just need to talk to you." I prayed that the earnestness in my voice would get through to him, if nothing else.

His brown eyes raked over my face. "Grace?" he asked in a thankfully quieter tone. "I don't know any Grace. Who are you, and what the bloody hell are you doing in my room?" His eyes ticked to the wet sheet. "You were *waterboarding* me?"

He rose to his feet slowly, the contours of his chest clearly visible beneath his wet shirt. He kept the gun steady in his hands.

"Only to wake you up!" I assured him.

"Are you a… vampire?" he asked, narrowing his eyes on me.

Crap. I really must have been looking deathly pale by now for his first guess to be a bloodsucker. I was about to respond when his expression darkened. "Oh, I know. I saw you in that cave. You were among the rebels who kidnapped my father."

"I was," I whispered.

I felt the blood drain from my face as I gazed up at him. So clueless. So oblivious. *Where do I even start? He doesn't remember a single thing…*

I could only think that, as with all stories, I ought to

start from the beginning.

"Will you sit down?" I asked quietly, realizing that I would find this a lot less intimidating without him towering over me. I was feeling so damn weak, so lethargic, since my last bout of tremors, it felt like a strain to hold my head tilted at this angle.

Lawrence hesitated. Then, keeping his gun aloft, he moved round the bed toward my side until he was standing behind me.

"Stand up," he commanded me.

I acquiesced.

"Remove your backpack."

I shrugged the bag off my shoulders and pushed it aside on the floor.

He strode in front of me, his brows deeply furrowed. His hands reached out and closed around my arms. His touch sent tingles down my spine as his palms traveled to my wrists before returning to the upper half of me. He continued to run his hands over my clothing, searching my back, chest and sides through my clothes. After inspecting my legs, from my thighs to my feet, he gestured to the mattress with a nod.

"I'll give you a minute to explain yourself," he said in a low voice. "Talk, *Ms. Novak.*"

I sank back onto the mattress, while he seated himself a safe distance away from me. His gun remained pointed at my chest.

The coldness in his eyes, the indifference, sent a chill stealing through me. Bracing myself, I ran my tongue over my cracked lower lip before beginning, "Have you ever heard of The Shade?"

He nodded. "Home to rebels with little to no respect for the work of the IBSI."

I smiled bitterly. *You got that right.*

"Well, you lived among us 'rebels' once, *Mr. Conway,*" I said. "And you got pretty comfortable on our island, too. You even begged us not to give you back to the IBSI when they came to reclaim you. You literally preferred to die than be handed back."

His mask cracked, his jaw twitching. I could tell that I had unnerved him, but there was still no sign of actual recognition in his eyes.

"We found you locked up in an underground bunker," I went on, "in The Woodlands. You had been heavily drugged, and lost all memory of your former life. Y-You looked about as sickly as I do now… I became your caregiver."

He cleared his throat, his right hand loosening and repositioning around the gun's handle. "I suggest you give me a strong reason to believe a word you're saying."

"For a start, I know your mother's full name. Georgina Susanna Conway."

His brows raised, but he didn't look too impressed. "That's hardly sufficient credibility for your story."

I was seconds from spitting out, *And I know she was murdered. By your cold-blooded brute of a father.* But somehow, I didn't think this was the right time to spill that yet. Lawrence was having enough trouble trusting my story as it was. He'd been so thoroughly brainwashed, I doubted he had it in him to believe his father could have been responsible for her death.

"I visited your grandparents," I proceeded. I figured my only option at this point was to keep hitting him with little pieces of information, keep planting little niggling doubts at the back of his mind that would eventually eat into his reason, even if any single piece of evidence I could offer him wasn't strong enough. It was agony to think how much easier this would have been if I'd just had a photograph of the two of us with me. "Lovely folks. Spencer and Angela Hulse. They own a pub called the Old Fox and live in Bristol, England. When was the last time you saw or spoke to them?" I asked, hoping to overwhelm him with my knowledge.

His lips cracked apart. Disturbance flashed in his eyes.

"You... You've been stalking my family?" he asked in a hushed voice.

"Yes," I replied, reluctant. "I guess I have."

My words had backfired on me. Instead of considering my message, the reason why I was telling him about my visit to his grandparents, his brain had gotten stuck on taking objection to a strange— apparently vampire—girl, stalking his family... which I guessed was fair enough.

His right hand clenched again around his gun and he rose to his feet.

But even as he stood armed before me, somehow, I still couldn't bring myself to feel afraid of him. But maybe that was just stupidity on my part. God knew, I had been known to be stupid before.

"Please, Lawrence," I urged, trying to keep my tone even, "will you just hear me out—"

He shook his head. Whatever window of openness I had seen in his eyes a few minutes before slammed shut. "How did you get in here?"

"Law—"

"Answer my question." It turned flat, uncompromising. Despite the difference in accents, it suddenly reminded me chillingly of his father's.

"The trap door, above the kitchen," I murmured.

"You need to leave," he said.

His forefinger glided over the trigger as I moved to appeal. "Leave," he repeated, glaring at me. His voice dropped deeper. "Before I change my mind about letting you leave at all."

He stepped backward, his left hand reaching for the door handle.

My desperation triggered a light to switch on in my brain.

"Wait," I breathed. "Just. Wait."

I rushed around the edge of the bed to where I had

dropped my backpack to the floor and rummaged inside it. *My notebook. Why didn't I think of that before?*

Grabbing the pink polka-dot notebook, I moved back to Lawrence.

From the look on his face as I had whirled on him, it seemed like he had been expecting me to withdraw a weapon. His eyes widened as I brandished the notebook.

"Take it," I hissed, shoving it toward his free left hand.

He clasped it. Staring down at the book, he hardly breathed.

Does this ring a bell in your head? Do you recognize it, even in the slightest?

"I want you to read it," I whispered, even as a bitter ache gripped my chest. I recalled the night we'd spent in that old abandoned castle—the last night we'd spent together—when I had been so hesitant to let him read what I'd written in this journal. Now here I was, urging him to take a peek.

I turned to the first page for him, remembering that my notes all referred to "Josh", rather than Lawrence. "I referred to you with a different name on these pages," I explained quickly, worried that he might immediately discount my notes. "I refer to you as Josh. Josh was the name you gave—"

"Josh." The name expelled from Lawrence's lips in a soft breath.

Hope surged through me as I searched his eyes. There was no sparkle of recollection within his irises as I had wished I'd see. Instead his eyes glazed over, as he whispered again, "Josh..."

Chapter 28: Lawrence

"Josh." My mother's brown eyes looked deep into mine as she spoke. "You'll remember that, won't you, darling? That's what we'll call you after we leave next week. But only for a little while. Just until we meet up with Deirdre."

I nodded, nestling deeper beneath the covers of my bed.

"Dad is busy on his trip, so he won't call before I return. Linda will be here to look after you."

I nodded again.

My mother leaned closer and planted a kiss over my forehead. Then she eyed her watch.

"Well, it's past your bedtime," she said, smiling. Mum's

smile always made me feel warm inside, but somehow tonight was different. It didn't seem like she was... really smiling.

"Why can't I come with you?" I asked.

"Sweetheart, it's only for a week. It will be gone in no time. Linda's got lots of exciting plans lined up for you. She's going to take you sledding tomorrow... Oh, and she's going to make your favorite crusty roasted potatoes for lunch."

I nodded, though, like my mother's smile, it didn't feel like I really meant it.

My mother kissed me again, on either side of my face. Then she rose from the edge of my bed and headed to the door. She pulled the door behind her so that it remained slightly ajar, creating a crack of light just how I liked it, before her footsteps disappeared down the hallway.

My breath hitched as my eyes refocused on the bright pink notebook in my hands.

The memory had washed over me, so searing and vivid, it was as though my mother's departure had happened only yesterday. That was the last memory I had of her—the last time I'd ever seen her before the accident—and I couldn't even recall the last time it had surfaced from the depths of my subconscious.

Josh.

The name this odd, pale girl had called me. That was what had brought it about.

Then something else tickled at the back of my mind. Another dusty memory, rising to the surface…

My father stood in the doorway of our home, where I had been expecting my mother to be standing two days earlier. He looked serious and tired as he clutched a pink, silk shawl in his hands. It looked just like one of my mother's shawls, one that always smelled of her perfume. But this one was ruffled and torn, frayed at the edges. That can't have been Mum's.

Surprised but elated by my father's unexpected visit, I left Linda's side and hurried toward him. He wasn't supposed to have come all the way to Scotland from America. Definitely not before Mum returned, and she and I had visited Deirdre.

He stepped in from the rain and bent down, gathering me to him as I wrapped my arms around him. He smelled of damp and cigarettes.

"How come you're here, Dad?" I asked.

I felt him gulp against my shoulder. He was being awfully quiet. He hadn't even said hello yet.

He carried me to the kitchen and sat me down in a chair. He seated himself next to me at the table. He was still holding the shawl tightly in his hand. His head dropped down. He looked sad. Sadder than I had ever seen him.

"Where's Mum?" I asked worriedly.

He still didn't talk.

I slid off my chair and tugged on his sleeve. "Dad? Where's Mum?"

Finally, he stopped being a statue. He looked at me with his sad eyes and replied, "You're going to return with me to America, Lawrence... Mom won't be coming back here."

I was barely even aware of the girl in front of me anymore. Or the room around me. My surroundings became invisible as my past washed over me.

After the first two memories—some of the earliest memories I possessed—I started remembering other things that I hadn't recalled in a long time. For some odd reason, my brain started ticking over the years that had followed my father's and my permanent departure from our second home in Scotland—a small renovated coastal castle—to America. I remembered how he had sold the place weeks after, how I had been forced to accept that we would never go back. How, in the weeks that followed, my father had finally told me what had happened to my mother. That she had been in an accident. There were blurs in my memory after that, during my pre-pubescent years. I supposed that grief and depression accounted for much of it. But one recollection remained with me: the persistent absence of my father after my mother's death.

My next most vivid memory was the year I started Creston Academy. My father had made an appearance on my induction day as he'd promised he would the last time I'd seen him, a couple of months before. I remembered the way he took me aside in the Academy's lobby and told me to work hard. That there would be brighter days ahead for me, for both of us. That I would see more of him as I got older. That we would become closer. He said that, once I had graduated, we could work together, and he was counting the days until that happened.

I moved into the Academy's accommodations and

spent the next string of my teenage years doing exactly as my father had advised me to do. Those were, indeed, brighter days. I became a happier person in that Academy. I was surrounded by more people my own age—no longer homeschooling, as I had been prior. The work was challenging and demanding, both physically and mentally. I threw myself into my study, and was second to none in my class. Whereas Creston Academy was a torture to be tolerated for many students, a place they looked forward to leaving every vacation, for me, it became a haven. My father visited me every few months or so—mostly we just spent an evening together, went out to dinner. One year leaked into the next until I was ready to graduate.

The graduation was due to take place in a large marquee among the Academy's training grounds. Of course, my father had given me his word he'd be there on such a momentous occasion. But as I tried to fast-forward to the graduation ceremony, again, I drew a blank. I couldn't remember anything past the morning I was preparing to leave for the event.

It was as though a wide chunk of my memory had just

been blotted out… wiped.

But… *Grace.*

That name was feeling more and more familiar to me by the moment. I experienced another tickling at the back of my brain. Tickling that was turning into an itch. *Grace. Grace.*

I stared at her pale, anxious face.

And then I remembered. Previously the blank in my memory had stretched from my graduation day up until I woke up in one of the Chicago HQ's labs… but now, I recalled waking up in a different place… before that.

I'd opened my eyes in an unfamiliar hospital room, with two strange women hovering over me. One middle-aged with tanned skin and chestnut-brown locks, and the other… yes. The other had been this girl. Grace. Though she'd looked very different then. She had looked like a normal, healthy young woman. Not like this sickly whitish creature.

The girl in front of me, Grace, was saying something to me now, but I wasn't comprehending. Her words didn't reach my brain as my eyes panned down to the notebook in my hands once again. This time, I began to read. Urgently, hurriedly, as though it would vanish from my grasp if I did not absorb the small, neat handwriting fast enough.

Wave after wave of *déjà vu* began rolling over me.

I knew the story unfolding over these notebook pages. The story of a girl—a kind, pretty girl—who had volunteered her days to assist a sickly boy bound to a wheelchair. A boy who had been sharp and snappy with her when he'd had no right to be. While she had remained attentive and patient. While she had lain in bed at night worrying about what the next day would bring for him. While she had looked for opportunities every minute of the day to bring a smile to his unhappy face. While she had defended and sheltered him during the most vulnerable time of his life.

This was a story of selflessness without conditions, of giving without bounds. A story of hope in darkness. Of strength in pain. Of friendship in strangers and… maybe even something more.

But the story ended too soon. Far too soon. The visit to the graveyard should have been only the beginning.

My hands shaking slightly, I raised my eyes to meet

the girl's. Grace Novak's. Her turquoise irises glistened as she gazed back at me. Hope surged behind them. Hope and relief.

I couldn't help but take in her ill appearance once again. Her pallid skin, her unnaturally protruding veins. I could practically feel the chill emanating from her body, even as we sat apart.

"Grace…" I breathed. "What *happened* to you?"

A weak smile formed on her dry lips as I spoke her name. She replied in a choked whisper, "The tables turned between us, Lawrence."

Chapter 29: Grace

No words could express the relief I experienced on witnessing Lawrence's remembrance. On having him look at me again like he knew me, like I was not an unwelcome stranger. When he spoke my name, I could hardly contain my emotions.

I almost didn't want to ruin this moment of reunion with him by informing him of what had happened to me. I wanted to wait just a few moments longer to relish this feeling of reconnection before marring it with horror.

But Lawrence's brown eyes were penetrating. He was

demanding answers. And time was slipping through our fingers.

He moved closer to me on the bed and raised a hand to my face. The sensation of his fingers—warm fingers—brushing against my cheek sparked an unexpected longing deep within me. I realized more than anything right now, I just wanted to hold him. I wanted to feel close to him again, to close the gap that time had wedged between us.

"God, you're freezing cold," he whispered, drawing his fingers away. "Grace, tell me what happened!"

"I was bitten," I replied in a strained voice. "Bitten and infected by two Bloodless."

"*Bloodless?*" he repeated, disbelieving. "Wha-How could you have been bitten by—"

Because I was an idiot… an idiot who went looking for you.

"After our visit to the graveyard, you suffered from a fit and lost consciousness," I replied. "We returned you to The Shade where you went downhill fast. In addition to your legs, you lost control of your arms. Then your father showed up." I felt sick to my stomach just thinking about Atticus. "He came to collect you, saying that he could heal you, and that if we didn't hand you back over to him, you would die." I paused to clear my throat, realizing just how dry and rough it had become. Noticing my discomfort, Lawrence rose from the bed and whipped to the cooler with supernatural speed, but of course, he found it empty.

I glanced at him sheepishly even as he eyed the empty glass bottles on the other side of his bed.

"Yeah... used them all up," I murmured. While we were on the subject, I couldn't help but ask, "*Why* on earth do you sleep like a dead person?"

He looked like the last thing he wanted to discuss right now was his sleep. "It's just... related to my, uh, transformation. The supplemental drugs I take affect me in weird ways."

I wanted to ask how he ever woke up, in that case, or whether waterboarding was a common method resorted to by his father, but as he reseated himself next to me, it was clear his mind had moved past the subject.

"Continue," he pressed.

"So we handed you over to your father, and that was

the last we saw of you," I went on, recalling the aftermath of Lawrence's departure. How I had stood on the jetty, watching his father's boat sail away into the distance. The hollowness that had gripped me...

"After you left, I was restless," I said. "I just couldn't leave things as they were... our investigation unfinished. So I-I continued on the path we'd begun and, well, that's how I wound up in so much trouble..."

Now I had the unsettling task of dealing with his request for details. But I didn't have the time or energy to go through every gory detail of the story now. Maybe I would have a chance to tell him later.

I had to communicate the essence in as short amount of time as possible and I figured I already knew the best place to start, even if it was the hardest...

Drawing in a deep breath, I steeled myself. "Lawrence," I said, eyeing him steadily. "I don't know how much you remember about your mother's death, but I have very strong reason to believe that it was not an accident."

His eyes bulged. "What?"

"I'm convinced your father had your mother

assassinated."

As he did a double-take, I hurried to explain about our discovery of FOEBA and all that had happened that led us to this conclusion. He was utterly speechless by the time I had finished my summary, all color drained from his face.

He clutched a trembling hand to his forehead, rubbing his temples before looking back at me, his face once again contorting with disbelief.

"Look, Lawrence," I breathed, reaching out and laying a gentle hand on his forearm. "I don't expect you to believe or accept everything I'm telling you now. I don't expect you to believe that your father murdered your mother. But one thing is an undeniable fact. For whatever reasons, the IBSI want the Bloodless to continue flourishing. The organization"—*or more specifically your father*—"is sitting on a cure to the Bloodless infection. They are stifling it. And I strongly believe that the reason you have been felling a certain type of tree here is because it has something to do with the antidote."

Lawrence suddenly shot up and darted to the window.

Gazing out at the whirling green smoke, he hissed a curse. "This gas…" he whispered. "It's designed to destroy trees."

"What?"

Lawrence exhaled sharply. "Assuming everything you've told me is accurate and none of your assumptions are misplaced, then my father has just let loose a toxic gas to weaken the trees."

I battled to express my shock and confusion. "Wha—? Why? H-How? B-But you've got these glass building things up in the trees! You're *living* up here! Why on earth would he do that?"

"The weakening is a gradual process," Lawrence explained. "The gas starts by drawing out moisture, shriveling up the leaves and killing them. The trunks and branches take longer to deteriorate—a few days. *Dammit!* That's why I was surprised when I realized he had unleashed it. I thought that we were going to try to avoid harming the natural environment of Aviary as much as possible while we worked to create a clearing for a new 'defense base'. The gas was only supposed to be a backup method for clearing trees, if we really started running behind on schedule. But now… all this means that he is planning to pack us up much sooner than anticipated."

"Oh, no," I gasped. I staggered to the window next to him, gazing out at the swirling vapor. "Lawrence, we've got to…"

My voice trailed off as Lawrence's attention shifted to the door. And then I realized why. Footsteps thudded in the corridor. It sounded like they were headed in our direction.

Before I could react, Lawrence kicked my backpack beneath the bed. His hands clutched my waist. He swept me off my feet and planted me down onto the bed. Then he lowered himself directly on top of me, his legs intertwining with mine, his elbows slightly propped up on either side of my head to create a small enclosure beneath him for me. His right hand slid down to my legs and curved them more at the knee—to make them less visible beneath the blanket, I assumed, more molded to his own form. My face level with his chest, he grabbed a pillow and positioned it above my head—and beneath his.

I would have mentioned that my father and Horatio could slip me away until the footsteps passed—whoever it was might just be traveling by this way with no intention of actually coming inside. But Lawrence had been too quick.

Now I lay sandwiched between his tense body and the mattress, trying not to breathe. His heartbeat, so close to my ear, quickened as the footsteps stopped outside his door. There was a click, then the sound of the handle turning. The door glided open and someone entered.

I supposed that from his or her angle by the door, it would look like Lawrence was simply lying on his stomach, if in a slightly odd elevated position. Hopefully not odd enough to draw notice.

There was a pause; I imagined whoever had entered was eyeing the bed. Then a voice spoke quietly. Atticus' voice. "You awake, Lawrence?"

Lawrence didn't respond, though I felt his biceps tense on either side of my head.

Atticus crossed the room and stopped again. A dull thud. It sounded like he'd laid something down on the dressing table. Then he was heading back to the door.

He paused again by the doorway before stepping out, the door shutting smoothly behind him.

Lawrence remained deathly still until Atticus' footsteps had disappeared. Thank God the man hadn't paid much attention to the empty bottles of water… or the damp patches on his son's bedding.

Lawrence shifted slowly, propping himself up higher on his elbows to glance down at me. Our gaze met. His lips and cheeks were flushed, his brown eyes alert and glistening with nerves.

"You okay?" he mouthed, breathing heavily.

I nodded.

His legs untwined from mine. He raised himself off me completely and climbed off the bed. His eyes settled nervously on the door again before returning to me.

He reached down a hand. I gripped it, his strong fingers closing around mine. He pulled me to sit upright—something that was becoming more and more of an effort to do by myself. My back and butt felt thoroughly wet now from the sheets, hardly helping with my already diminishing temperature.

I glanced at the dressing table. A gas mask sat on its

surface, along with a note.

"What does it say?" I whispered.

Lawrence picked it up. "'You will need this to step outside from now on. And a change of plan: we will be packing up sooner than expected. Buzz me tomorrow.'"

Anxiety returned to me full force. "The trees," I gasped. I could only assume this meant Atticus had decided to wipe them all out in one blow.

I staggered to the window, pressing my palms flat against it and gazing out hopelessly. "Is there no way to stop this gas?" I whispered, recalling how quickly my father, Horatio and I had witnessed it spreading through the area. I wouldn't have been surprised if by now it had reached all the surrounding jungle for miles and miles.

"Not that I know of," he replied. "I mean, it's been released already. There's no calling it back."

Oh, no. No, no, no.

My father cleared his throat behind us. As Lawrence and I turned, he and Horatio had manifested.

"Wha-What on earth..." Lawrence exclaimed. His eyes darted to me in confusion.

"Meet my father, Benjamin Novak," I said, realizing

that I had never introduced the two before. "And this is one of our jinni friends, Horatio Drizan. They're the ones who helped me inside here… Sorry, I lied to you about my entrance through the trap door. While I was still a stranger to you, I didn't think you could handle seeing them."

Lawrence eyed them one after the other.

"Apologies for the intrusion," my father said briskly, stepping forward and reaching out a hand. Lawrence shook it uncertainly. "But on the most urgent matter of the trees," my father went on, "we witnessed the IBSI smuggling them back through the portal. They were loading them into a cargo ship. Many of them. So they've taken a stock. You must be aware of that, surely, as one of the main showrunners here?"

Lawrence nodded. "Yes, uh… my father wished for us to keep some. He didn't give me a clear explanation as to why. Just said to transport some back. We loaded up a cargo ship bound for Sri Lanka. The IBSI has a base there, though it mostly serves as storage for weapons and other large equipment."

"Sri Lanka," my father repeated, wetting his lower lip.

He looked to me. "Then maybe not all is lost, Grace. Even if, as Lawrence indicates, these jungles will be ruined, they've kept aside a stock of the trees. A large stock. I'm sure it wouldn't be impossible to figure out how to either hijack the ship on its way to Sri Lanka, or reclaim some of the trees once they reach there... So this is not our main problem. Our main problem is we still don't know how these trees factor into the Bloodless antidote. We *need* the formula."

"Clearly Lawrence has no idea what it is," Horatio said, raising his brows at Lawrence as if for confirmation.

Lawrence shook his head, frowning. "No. The first time I heard of FOEBA was only this evening, from Grace."

"Atticus has—" I choked mid-sentence. To my horror, I spiraled into a coughing fit. Drops of blood sprayed from my mouth, staining my palms and the gray carpet. Shocked, Lawrence raced to fetch a tissue. My father gripped my shoulders and sat me back down on the bed. Lawrence bent over me, dabbing the blood from my lips.

"Christ," Lawrence murmured.

I closed my eyes tight, taking a moment to breathe in deeply. The last thing I wanted right now was to descend into another fit in front of Lawrence.

"What my daughter was about to say," my father whispered tensely, "is that your father has—or at least had—your mother's files cracked open on his laptop. Those files must contain details of the antidote, or the IBSI would not be so bent on guarding them. Lawrence…" My father rose to his feet, leveling with Lawrence eye to eye. "We need your help. Not only Grace, but *the world* needs your help. The IBSI is sitting on a way to eradicate the Bloodless problem, a problem the organization supposedly works day in and day out to solve. Clearly, it's all just a front. They're using the presence of the Bloodless as an excuse to maintain their iron grip over the government. Because think about it. Without the prevalence of Bloodless, what can they actually offer? They have hardly proven effective at combating other supernatural creatures. Bloodless are the only species they're fully capable of protecting humanity against—with their mutants patrolling borders. The Bloodless are the primary reason why the world believes they need the IBSI so much." My father reached out and clutched Lawrence's shoulder. Gripping it hard, he went on, "You're on the inside, Lawrence. As inside as a person can get. You are the son of the IBSI's leader. If you don't uncover and expose the truth, nobody will... You need to finish what your mother started. You need to take up her mantle and fight. You need to make sure that her death was not in vain."

A chill silence descended on the room as my father finished.

Lawrence's face had turned ashen, gray. My heart went out to him. This was all so much for him to take in within the space of an evening. Hearing that his mother had been murdered by his father was enough to shock anybody into a stupor, not to speak of all the other bombshells we'd dropped on his shoulders.

I also feared for him. I feared what would happen should he take my father's words to heart—should he become a rogue agent in the IBSI, betray his father and embark on a mission to expose to the world what his mother and her accomplices had attempted to reveal. What if he met with the same fate as her before he ever managed to accomplish it? I didn't doubt for a second that Atticus would target Lawrence if he was given reason to suspect he was a threat.

One thing was for certain. This would be a dangerous game, should Lawrence begin to play it.

I suspected such thoughts were going through his mind. He backed away from my father, his hands balling into fists, and roamed slowly about the room. Horatio, my father and I didn't speak a word as we let him mull things over.

Then Lawrence returned to where we waited on the other side of the bed. He drew in a deep breath as he stopped before my father. But, even as he addressed him, his eyes fixed on me. "Mr. Novak, I will do all that I can to get to the bottom of this. I… I have only your and Grace's word to go by that my father is indeed responsible for all that you have charged him with. But one way or another, whether you are right or wrong, whether or not he did indeed murder my mother, I will not rest until I uncover the truth… The full truth."

"You've made the right decision, Lawrence," my father replied.

I bit down on my lip as I gazed up at Lawrence, my heart singing with gratitude. He left my father's side and bent down, until his face was level with mine. He reached out to brush his fingers against my cheek again, and then felt my forehead. Worry marred his face.

"And I know that you need an answer soon," he said in a softer voice, as though his words were only meant for me to hear.

"But be careful, Lawrence," I whispered back. "Don't do anything stupid."

He raised his brows. "Says the girl who risked her life, many times over, to uncover my mother's secret? Surely I owe you this much, even leaving aside the care you gave me on your island."

"But if you get caught—" I began.

He nodded, his eyes intense and dead serious as they bored into mine. "I think by now, I can make an educated guess about what will happen if I get caught."

I nodded back at him. "Right," I managed, pursing my lips.

We held each other's gazes for a moment longer before he slowly returned to his full height.

"I'll begin the moment you leave." He addressed my father.

My father nodded, then turned his focus on me. He stooped down and picked me up, carrying me in his arms. "Then we shall leave now," he said. "There are a number of tasks we need to carry out ourselves, like reclaiming those trees and bringing them to The Shade for safety... How will you let us know of your findings, Lawrence? It would be too risky for you to make contact via telephone or other electronic means, in case anybody within the IBSI found out or had you monitored."

"Oh, of course," Lawrence said. "I'll have to find a way to visit in person."

"If you suspect you'll leave Aviary as soon as tomorrow due to your father's change of plans and this release of gas," I said, "where will you go? Will you return to Chicago?"

"Most likely," Lawrence said, "at least initially... But I need to think things through before I can give any definite answers."

"But you know where The Shade is, right?" I asked anxiously. Nothing would be worse than to have him discover the cure only to not reach us in time due to having no clear information about our island's exact location.

"That kind of information won't be difficult to gain from the IBSI," my father responded. "They know very well where our island is. They just can't get inside it."

"Right," Lawrence said, gritting his teeth. "Finding the island is the least of my worries."

We all fell quiet again. Then my father exchanged glances with Horatio. I sensed that the jinni was seconds from vanishing us away from here… but something leapt up inside me as I fixed my eyes on Lawrence for what could be the last time.

"Wait," I breathed, clutching my father's arms and lowering myself to the floor.

"Wait for what?" my father asked. "Grace, we all need to get a move on."

"I know," I whispered, taking a step closer to Lawrence as he stood rooted to the spot, staring at me. "I just… I just need you to wait… a few moments more."

I stopped a couple of inches in front of Lawrence, my

head tilted up to his face.

I wasn't even sure what I was doing. I wasn't sure why I had told my father and Horatio to wait, when all we needed was to leave and for Lawrence to start work as soon as he possibly could. I was fading away by the hour, for God's sake.

But something inside me just... couldn't stand to leave yet. Not quite yet...

My mouth feeling dry again, my hands seemed to move of their own accord as they reached to clutch Lawrence's. I raised his hands gently to my lips and placed a soft kiss on each one.

Lawrence's mouth parted. I wondered if he felt as short of breath as I did in that moment.

I was becoming less and less aware of my father and Horatio's presence behind us as I raised my arms and rested them over Lawrence's shoulders. I pulled myself closer against him, burying my head against the crook of his neck. His hands lowered chastely to my waist.

I closed my eyes as I embraced him, trying to shut out the rest of the world completely, all my worries, all my fears. I fought to focus only on this very moment, while

I had Lawrence in my arms. While his strength and warmth surrounded me. While my limbs relaxed into him and our hearts beat as one.

As I treasured Lawrence's embrace, for some reason it was Orlando's words that echoed in my mind. The words he had spoken seconds before he had leaned forward and kissed me.

"I have *to live in the now."*

Holding Lawrence, I suddenly understood exactly how Orlando had been feeling then. I experienced his same train of thought. I felt the same urge, the same impulse… the same abandon that he must have felt toward me to have claimed what he did.

Who knows if I will be even be alive tomorrow? Who knows if Lawrence will be? He might not last longer than a few hours as a double agent. The IBSI must have measures in place to weed out such rogues.

I raised my head from Lawrence's chest and took in his face. It bore an expression of mild confusion, yet also steadiness. Stillness. As though he, too, had managed to withdraw his mind from all other places and make himself present nowhere else but in this moment with me. I wanted to lose myself in the calmness of his irises. But then he distracted me by allowing his gaze to wander momentarily to my lips.

That small movement on Lawrence's part—a betrayal that his thoughts were reflecting my own—became my undoing. Confidence surged within me. I fixed my gaze on his lips, his firm, yet soft lips, leaving him with no doubt as to my state of mind. Then I closed my eyes and instinct took over the rest. My lips moved to his first. They wandered from one corner of his mouth to the other, exploring its contours and leaving behind a trail of soft almost-kisses. Our breathing an uneven symphony, our mouths centered and touched. Then our lips closed together, as if they had been molded to each other's shape. I kissed him the way I had wanted to deep down that night in the old derelict hotel. It was how I'd always imagined a first kiss should be. Like a thousand fireworks erupting in my chest at once. Like my heart might explode from the speed at which it raced. Like I could take on an army of Bloodless. Like I would never feel afraid of anything again… Like all was right with the world in this moment. This perfect moment.

When our lips unlocked, my vision felt hazy, my brain intoxicated. I couldn't think of anything but the desire to lean in and feel his lips against mine again. From the glassy look in Lawrence's eyes, I knew that he was buzzing with the same passion, the urge to taste me once more.

And we would have succumbed to our longing.

But reality knocked on our door too soon.

Chapter 30: Lawrence

"Grace." Her father's voice broke through our halo. "We've got to leave."

I was feeling heady as I gazed down at Grace through hooded eyelids. Even now, in her ill state, she looked beautiful to me. Her light still shone through those turquoise irises of hers.

I hadn't been expecting any of this. I'd been expecting her to vanish with her father and the jinni the moment after her father picked her up. My heart had hammered like a drum as she approached me. As she wrapped her arms around my neck, I couldn't quite believe what was happening. Then things spiraled out of control; I was barely aware of the fact I was kissing a girl whose father stood a few feet behind her. After her lips pressed against mine, my entire body responded to that kiss. I was lost to her.

I had never gotten close to a girl before. All dealings with the opposite sex had been perfunctory. They had never been a priority in my schedule, in my strict routine. But this girl… She was something special.

When her father beckoned her away from me, I didn't want to let go of her waist. I wanted to raise my hands and run my fingers through her hair. Brush my thumbs against her cheeks. Dip down to feel her lips against mine again.

But she had to leave. She had to leave this place, and she had to leave me. We both had our own separate obstacles before us now. I had to somehow uncover a decade-old mystery, while she had to somehow survive until I managed it.

The jinni took Grace's backpack and notebook, while her father picked her up again. Her eyes, their corners moistened, remained on me.

"Good luck, Lawrence," she breathed. Her lips, flushed from my kiss, trembled slightly.

"Good luck," I managed, my voice as rough as a smoker's. I could barely even bring myself to glance at her father during these last precious moments...

Then she disappeared. She, her father and the jinni. I was left standing alone in the small box room. I stared out of the window at the smoke-choked jungle. Hollowness began seeping into me, the euphoria of Grace's kiss slowly ebbing away, my breathing returning to normal, my heart resuming its normal pace. The only evidence that Grace had been here was the damp sheets and the empty water bottles.

I tried to pry my thoughts away from Grace. I had to if I wanted to regain a semblance of concentration.

Everything she and her father had told me during their visit replayed in my mind.

Could my father really have killed my mother? His own wife?

Could he have lied to me for all these years?

What else had he lied to me about? Why did I still have a blank space in my memory? What had actually happened during that period of time from the day of my graduation until I woke up in The Shade? Had I really volunteered for the drug trial?

I wished that I could just talk to my father, look him in the eye and ask him my questions man to man. But of course, I couldn't do that. As much as I was fighting against it, too large a part of me suspected that he was guilty of everything Grace said he was.

I couldn't say anything. I had to act the same as when he'd left me earlier that evening. I had to pretend that nothing was wrong, that there wasn't a storm within me, ripping me apart. And I had to remain his obedient son, his puppet… at least until I had discovered all I needed to know.

Time and distance had forged a gap between my father and me ever since my mother had died. Now, after I'd been woken up from the experiment that I had apparently volunteered for, he felt like a stranger to me. Although, as he had promised all those years ago, we had started working closely together, I still felt miles apart from him. Further away than I had in my childhood, when he'd been on the other side of the globe for months at a time. He was a stranger. Disconnected. Unpredictable.

If he had it in him to assassinate his wife, what would stop him from doing the same to his son?

I staggered backward, the backs of my legs hitting the bed post. I sank down on the mattress.

I had no idea how this was going to play out. How long I would even survive after embarking on this dangerous course… I could only recall Benjamin Novak's last words as I sat there in the darkness.

If I don't uncover and expose the truth, nobody will.

CHAPTER 31: BEN

I felt shaken after witnessing my daughter and Lawrence kiss. I hadn't known they had grown so close. I'd thought all they'd shared was friendship... though those were famous last words.

As we traveled among the treetops, away from the IBSI's temporary setup in Aviary city, I put off asking Horatio to vanish us the rest of the way back to the portal. I wanted to see if we could spot, and hopefully sabotage, hunters setting off more gas.

As we soared, protected by the vacuum Horatio had reset around us, I glanced down at my daughter. Her head rested against my shoulder, her eyes unfocused.

"Are you okay?" I asked softly, even though it was a stupid and probably insensitive question. There was very little that could possibly be "okay" about my daughter right now. I just wanted her to say something. She was being disconcertingly quiet.

"Mm," she murmured, her eyes still averted from mine.

I refocused my own attention on where it ought to be, tracing the ground beneath us.

I had told my father that we wouldn't be gone long. I realized now that we had been gone longer than I had intended. I had to pray that our visit to Lawrence would prove fruitful.

I sensed goodness in Lawrence's eyes the way I didn't in his father's. Perhaps he took after his mother more. I sensed honesty and determination, a desire to do what was right. Qualities he would need if he was to stand a chance of succeeding.

I had no way of knowing how strongly he felt for my daughter, how much emotion had been packed behind his kiss. But he knew that there was more hanging in the balance than Grace's life. We had turned his life upside down with the revelation of his mother's murder—assuming he believed it. There was no way he could simply continue living his life like before, cooperating with his father. Unless he was a cold-hearted bastard after all.

Leaving aside Grace, that alone should ensure that he did his best to get to the bottom of this mystery. We just had to hope that his best would be enough.

We soon arrived back in the area surrounding the portal without having spotted any hunters along the way. The gas had become thick in this area by now, too.

On reaching the tree where we'd left our group, to our dismay, it was empty.

The three of us exchanged glances. There was deep concern in Horatio's eyes, but I tried not to immediately assume the worst. "Maybe they had to shift away from this smoke," I said. We still didn't know how toxic it was for normal, physical beings. I hadn't given Grace a chance to find out because I had asked Horatio to put up protection around us before she'd had a chance to breathe much in.

"Where would they have gone?" Grace croaked.

"I wonder if they could be taking shelter on the other side of the portal," Horatio suggested.

"Then we should check," I said.

The three of us piled in through the portal, letting the vacuum suck us down in a spiral at breakneck speed through the star-strewn abyss. I got the same feeling of déjà vu each time I traveled through one of these things, and found myself gazing beyond the misty tunnel wall, wondering if I might ever spot another fae. I still wasn't sure what happened to the one who'd given me my body. Sherus, his name was. The last time I'd seen him, he'd been preparing for a clash with the ghouls atop a snowy mountain in Canada. We weren't sure of the outcome of the battle; I hadn't heard from or come across him—or thankfully any of those wretched ghouls—since.

We arrived on the other side, shooting out into the forested area that bordered the IBSI's Bermuda base.

"Ben!" a female voice hissed barely a few seconds after we had emerged.

Safi rushed toward us through the trees.

Safi? What on earth…

"Where are Lucas and Kailyn?" the jinni asked before I could even open my mouth. "They found you?"

"Huh? What are you talking about? I haven't seen Lucas and Kailyn."

She cussed beneath her breath, flapping her arms by her sides. Safi was older than Aisha, and more mature in many ways, but her mannerisms reminded me of her on occasion. "Lucas came to fetch us from The Shade," she began to explain hurriedly. "He fetched a whole group of us. Jinn, vamps, wolves, the usual motley crew. But we didn't last more than a few minutes on the other end. The green smoke paralyzed everyone except for the fae and jinn. And then we found a bunch of your group passed out. River, your mom, sister, Caleb, all of them. We took them all back through the portal on Lucas' suggestion. And we ended up just taking them back to The Shade where they could recover more comfortably. You, Grace, Horatio and Derek weren't among them, though. So Lucas and Kailyn stayed back to look for you. The reason I'm still here is because I stayed back to keep an eye on this end of the gate."

She'd been speaking so fast, it took a few seconds for everything she'd said to register in my brain.

Tensing my jaw, I settled Grace on the ground and held her shoulders. "I'm returning to Aviary to help with the search. Safi will take you back to The Shade… won't you, Safi?"

Safi nodded. "All right."

To my relief, Grace didn't argue. She nodded, docile. I supposed she had realized that she had done all that she could. She'd spoken to Lawrence and she would have to have faith that he would pull through.

Grace climbed onto Safi's back and the jinni vanished with her, leaving Horatio and me to return through the portal.

As we sped back through the vacuum, I couldn't stop the fear from gripping me. My father. Why hadn't he been found among the rest of the group?

Where on earth could he have gotten to?

Chapter 32: Lucas

"Ugh. Where the hell are they?" I hissed to Kailyn. My nerves were fraying and this blasted jungle heat was doing nothing to help my temperament. As capable as I was of wielding fire, I couldn't stand this level of humidity. And it wasn't like we could thin ourselves either. We needed to stay at least somewhat visible to make it possible for one of the missing to spot us.

We had been searching for miles through these jungles, looking for Ben, Grace, Horatio and my brother, all the while witnessing the leaves of the trees surrounding us wither before our very eyes—the smoke seemed to be affecting all green plant life, not just the peach-colored trees.

It felt like we would be searching for a hundred miles more before we ever found them. It was like they had just… vanished.

"Maybe we should return to the portal," Kailyn muttered, wiping a sheen of sweat from her brow with the back of her hand. "It's possible that they found their way back and have already returned to Bermuda."

I supposed that was a possibility. In any case, I was out of ideas and patience. "All right," I said, exhaling in frustration. "Let's head back."

We turned back on ourselves and whizzed through the toxic fog. But we didn't make it as far as the portal. We crossed paths with Ben and Horatio as we reached the clearing where the IBSI kept their machinery. Now, I could hardly make out the machinery through the smog.

Ben gazed from me to Kailyn, wide-eyed and worryingly expectant.

Then the same question blurted from my mouth and his simultaneously:

"Where's your father?"

"Where's my father?"

We gaped at each other, our jaws dropping.

"He's not with you?" Ben asked in an almost accusatory tone. A tone I really did not appreciate in this moment.

"No! He's not with us!" I shot back. "We thought he was with you!"

The four of us stared at each other, speechless for several moments.

"Maybe he returned through the portal," Kailyn said. "Like I suggested before."

"No," Ben replied. His throat sounded tight with worry. "He hasn't."

"How do you know that?" I asked him. "Where have you guys been?"

"We went with Grace to find Lawrence," Ben replied, "But that's a long story. We just came from the other side of the portal—we spoke to Safi. She's returned to The Shade with Grace now, but she has no idea where my father is."

Oh, great. That's. Just. Great. I supposed I ought to feel grateful that at least we could cross Ben, Horatio and

Grace off our list of missing persons… But my brother still being lost hardly allowed me to appreciate the relief.

"So we have to keep looking," Kailyn said firmly. "He must be on this side of the portal, in Aviary, if he hasn't passed through."

"Keep looking *where*?" I whispered, gazing cluelessly around the treetops. "He could be anywhere in this place."

"Maybe the hunters got him," Horatio said in a low tone. He voiced what we were all too afraid to think of.

My fists clenched. I sure hoped that Horatio was wrong. If the hunters had found Derek, I doubted that he would still be alive by now, after everything my brother had led the League to do in The Woodlands and The Trunchlands…

"We just have to keep moving," Ben urged. "And we should split up again. You and Kailyn stick together, I'll go with Horatio."

And so we parted ways, either party turning in opposite directions. Kailyn and I continued forging ahead through the sweltering heat in search of him.

Hold on, little brother. Wherever you are, hold on…

Chapter 33: Derek

My head felt close to exploding as consciousness slowly returned to my brain. I became aware of a strong gust of wind blowing over me, prickling the hairs on my arms. Beneath me was something sharp.

Lifting my eyelids felt like the fight of my life. As my vision came into focus, directly above me was a ceiling made of jagged rock, uneven walls surrounding either side of me. I was lying on layers of twigs. Layers that were molded in a curved fashion, like the shape of a giant basket... or a nest.

What the...

I flinched as I struggled to raise my head. It felt like a brick. A splitting headache seared in my skull. Sitting upright, I spotted the source of the light that trickled into the cave—an oval entrance that looked out over an ocean of trees.

I rubbed my head and blinked rapidly, trying to remember what the heck had just happened. *The green gas. That's right. Then the choking. The blackout.* It was clear here; the air smelt pure. I supposed that was why I had woken up in the first place; the effects of whatever that smoke was must have faded.

I glanced down at my arms and the rest of my body. My pants were thoroughly torn, and as for my shirt, I might as well have been wearing none.

Gripping the edge of the strange bed of twigs, I slid myself out of it before standing on unsteady feet. Slowly, I approached the entrance. I stopped just before the sun's rays could hit me directly. Outside was a narrow ledge. I was among the heights of one of Aviary's mountain ranges.

God. What happened to everyone else? Sofia. She had been right next to me. And Rose. Vivienne. Almost every one of my family members had been with me in that tree. *Why am I alone now?* That was somehow a more chilling thought than how I had gotten up here in the first place.

I grimaced as I stared out at the sunny landscape. Being human would have come in handy. I could have begun my descent down the mountain without fear of being burnt to a crisp. But it seemed I would have no choice.

I had to find the others.

Steeling myself, I swept out of the cave and into the sunlight. The rays immediately dug into me like lasers. But I had experienced this agony before. More times than I could count. *It's nothing I can't handle. I just have to get to the ground.* Once I had reached the foothills and reentered the jungle, it would be easy to find shade. Though I had to avoid that smoke again at all costs. Hopefully, it wouldn't have spread so far.

My skin frying, sweat dripped from my hairline as I began lowering myself down the face of the cliff as fast as my still-unsteady limbs could manage.

Then I heard a familiar sound.

A resounding, deep-throated squawking coming from somewhere above me. I recognized that noise from when I had been waiting among the treetops with my family. It had blasted overhead.

Something told me that I did not want to look up.

Instead, I cast my eyes downward at the steep drop that still remained beneath me. Squinting in the sunlight, I attempted to gauge where I might land while keeping injuries to a minimum, since the foothills were spiky and uneven.

As the squawking multiplied and grew closer—I suspected at least two creatures to be above me—I let go of the cliff and went hurtling down in a gut-clenching freefall.

My feet touched down amid a pile of rocks, the force of the landing sending a tremor from the soles of my feet up to my skull. I bit my tongue against the pain of the sun's rays as I raced forward, my vision tunneling in on the borders of the jungle.

But as fast as I raced, before I could reach the beginning of the trees, broad wings fluttered across my vision. The next thing I knew, a giant feathered bird had planted itself in front of me, blocking off my path. Its beak was long and hooked at the end, perfectly engineered for tearing into meat. Its wide wings were as green as envy, its eyes were slanted and beady black. One of the many dangerous resident species here in Aviary. Apparently, I was its meal.

Extending my claws, I lashed out. It screeched as I caught the tender flesh of its rounded breast, creating a line of blood. But it in no way relented. Then a second feathered beast dropped down next to it, almost identical in size. The two beat their wings, creating a dust storm, before swooping down on me at once with speed no ordinary bird would possess. Their gnarled talons wrapped around my shoulders and arms. I couldn't fight them off before they beat their mighty wings and raised me into the sky.

These must have been my "saviors". The birds must have found me after falling unconscious from the green gas among the trees. They'd taken me back to their lair in the mountaintops... But I couldn't understand why they hadn't killed me already. I was a vampire, after all. I would've thought, after what Cruor did to this realm, every species would be instinctively opposed to vampires.

I continued struggling and thrashing in vain as the birds soared with me exactly the way I'd just come, up the mountainside. They touched back down outside the cave. When they released me, I dropped to the ground and immediately lurched to leap off the cliff again, but they closed in on me before I could, cornering me against the entrance and making it clear they wanted me back in the cave.

I tried to lurch forward again and slip through the gap between my two unwanted wardens. I needed another chance to dive down the mountain and reach the jungle, where I would have a better chance of escaping from them, finding somewhere to hide. But I didn't even make it to the edge of the small plateau. The second bird, whose beak was tinged reddish, grabbed me with a single talon and shoved me roughly toward the entrance of the cave.

I reluctantly acquiesced, backing just a little into the cave, only so that I could get a brief reprieve from the sun. I felt utterly confused as I stared at my two captors.

They were still making no move to dig into me, tear me apart. They just wanted me in this cave. Maybe they planned to save me for dinner.

The red-backed bird fluttered its heavy wings and clicked its beak, drawing me still further inside.

I had two choices now. Continue my attempts to get past them, or obey their wishes and remain at the back of this cave, and wait.

I didn't think that I could suffer the latter, so I tried five times more to steal through the gaps between and on either side of them, but each time was a failure. They were both four times my size, and managed to grab me and thrust me back to the cave every time. These strange wardens were not letting me go. So, as much as it killed me, I wasn't sure what else I could do but obey, and reseat myself on the twig nest at the back.

"What the hell are you playing at?" I grunted in frustration. Of course, these were not the supernatural creatures we called Hawks, so they could not respond to me. These birds, as sharp as they were, were still animals.

I found myself gazing around the interior of the cave, hoping to spot any kind of hole, or crack, or *something* that I could slip into to escape. There was nothing. Just solid, jagged walls of rock. The only way out was ahead, and they remained protecting it like guards.

It being cooler back here, at least I was in less pain. My fried skin had already begun to heal.

I tried to steady my breathing and calm my mind. Perhaps I would just have to play their game for a while. Whatever this game was exactly. Maybe I would even have to wait until they fell asleep, or at least one of them rested, making my chances of escape less slim.

If only I had my fire...

And so I waited. My eyes never leaving the birds, I watched for even the slightest moment of weakness, of inattentiveness.

I saw my chance sooner than expected. I had no way of telling the time, but I suspected less than an hour had passed. The birds ruffled their feathers and, to my surprise, took off into the air at once. It was like they had gotten bored of waiting, lost interest in me. Not skipping a beat, I leapt from the nest and darted to the entrance, the sun once again piercing my skin and impairing my vision. But I barely felt the pain. Relief overwhelmed me as I raced to the edge of the cliff. I was about to leap off when a voice spoke.

"Hold your stance." It was a scratchy male voice.

I froze. Taking one step back away from the edge and turning slowly, I found myself standing face-to-face with a group of men, who looked almost human except for the wings sprouting from the backs of their shoulders and sharp beaks where their noses and mouths should have been.

A flood of memories washed over me. Of all the supernatural creatures I had come across in recent years, during missions with the League, I had not seen a Hawk for decades. I believed the last one I'd seen in the flesh had been my father-in-law, Aiden, before the witches had managed to sort him out. That was when Rose and Ben were still children.

"Who are you?" I asked.

"My name is Tidor, second cousin of Arron the Great," the man standing closest to me at the front of the group responded. His eyes were coral in color, his wispy hair dark brown.

Arron the Great. I grimaced internally. That Hawk

had been many things, but great wasn't one of them. I despised the man, even after his death, given his history with my family, The Shade and Earth in general. Though I should have been at least a little grateful to him, I supposed, for having provided my son with a vial of liquid that ended up saving his soul—even if that had not been the Hawk's intention.

"And are you responsible for bringing me here?" I asked, even as I found it odd that he didn't ask me my name in return. I got the sense that they already knew exactly who I was, recognized me somehow, even though I was sure I had never met these Hawks personally.

"Not exactly," Tidor replied. "Although the two birds who carried you here are our scouts—our foragers and spies, ever since the humans set foot in Aviary."

I raised a brow while shuffling back to stand beneath the shade of the cave's entrance to save my boiling skin. "You are so afraid to forage and spy yourselves that you send your pets in your place?" I asked. "Are you so afraid of mere humans?"

Tidor's face darkened. "They are not mere humans," he responded, clipped.

I supposed he was right. More and more of the hunters these days were being injected with whatever powerful drug they had developed that caused them to become fast and tough like supernaturals.

"In addition, they have brought with them fire-breathing mutants," Tidor added.

Ah, yes. Those cuddly things.

Still, the Hawks ought to at least *try*.

"But they are invading your homeland," I countered. "You might be weakened and diminished in numbers—as I have heard—but have you no pride left for your country? No courage?"

Tidor's coral eyes narrowed, as if he was incensed by my words. "I suggest you keep such questions to yourself if you wish to remain with your neck intact."

As intimidating as their appearance was, I wasn't afraid of them. I found it difficult to experience fear for men who wouldn't even attempt to hold their own ground.

"How many of you are left?" I couldn't help but ask. "And where do you live now that your city has been overtaken?"

"We abandoned that city long ago," Tidor spat, still seething from my insult. "And it is none of your business how many of us are left."

I frowned at him, then cast my eyes over the stretch of jungle beneath us. I shrugged and let out a sigh. "Well, since you seem to have no interest in conversing with me, I wonder why you had your pets scoop me up in the first place? And why me?" I added, my mind returning to my family. I had been hoping that the Hawks would not have been so hostile. As much as I distrusted them, I desperately needed to find my family. Flying would be the best and fastest way to do that, especially if the jungles were still blanketed with that toxic smoke. I wouldn't be able to travel on foot if they were—at least not for long. But I wasn't sensing any leeway with these Hawks, so it didn't seem like I had a choice but to venture out alone.

"Our foragers were searching for food," Tidor replied. "Not that your vampire flesh is worthy of eating... for us, anyway," he added. "I suppose you caught their eye as the largest piece of meat."

I held Tidor's glare a few moments longer, then

turned my back on them all, even as I wondered if they would try to stop me. "Well," I muttered beneath my breath. "I won't take up your precious time any longer. You obviously have far more pressing matters to attend to than the invasion of your country…"

Leaving my words hanging in the air, for the second time in the span of a few minutes I was about to leap from the cliff. But I found myself stalling yet again as a different Hawk cleared his throat and spoke up. "Wait." He was the Hawk who'd been standing on the right side of Tidor. He shared the same murky brown hair, though his eyes were closer to yellow than coral. "I am Killian," he said, stepping forward. "And I must say what my brother is too proud to say." Tidor scowled, looking anywhere but in my direction. I looked this new Hawk deep in the eyes. *Brother of Tidor.*

"Perhaps you will then also explain to me the reason why you have kept a vampire like myself alive?" I said. "I assume you were aware of my presence before I woke, and were waiting for me to come to."

Killian nodded, glancing furtively at his brother.

"We have heard," he began, "via acquaintances in

other lands, what you and your comrades did to these human brutes in both The Woodlands and The Trunchlands… Novak," he said, resentment in his tone, "We are weak. Weaker than you might think. There are several hundred of us left, but although our bodies might look intact and capable of war… our minds are not."

I crossed my arms over my chest, scrutinizing the man in front of me. I knew desperation in a person's eyes when I saw it, and this Hawk's were swimming in it.

"Go on," I said.

Killian swallowed. "Since Arron died, our people have lost faith. There is no single Hawk among us—neither myself nor Tidor—who commands the respect required of a leader. Of a commander to lead them to battle. Since Arron's death, every one of us has migrated to the northernmost tip of Aviary, where we live simply to survive. None of us has ever shown the competence that Arron once showed. And all of our other leaders who commanded respect alongside him died many years ago in the war that wrecked our spirits. As much as my brother and I have attempted to find ways to embolden them again, we have…" His voice trailed off as he exhaled heavily. "We have no sway among them." Killian's fists clenched at the admission. Tidor looked like he wanted to punch his brother, yet apparently as much as he despised the truth, by his silence, he agreed with every word.

I frowned deeply. "So, uh… what are you saying, exactly?"

Killian looked like he was wincing, though sometimes it was hard to make out a Hawk's true expression given their lack of nose and mouth. But his voice was as tight as a knot as he replied, "You are a leader, Novak. And you have proven yourself competent more than once in ridding countries of these vermin. Just as we know of this, so do our people."

My jaw dropped.

Had I really understood correctly what he was implying? Was he really suggesting that the only man capable of rousing his populace to defend their own country was… a vampire?

My mind spun. I couldn't even wrap my head around the notion. *Either I've misunderstood, or the world has gone insane.*

"I'm afraid you're not making yourself clear, Hawk," I said tersely.

"Just spit it out," Tidor said, his chest heaving with aggravation.

Killian's voice became shaky. "I'm asking you, *King Derek*, to become a leader to our people. To rouse them, and lead them to battle—a battle we should have fought the moment we detected these humans on our soil."

Okay.

Maybe I'm the one going insane.

I was lost for words for almost a minute as I stared at the Hawks, wondering whether this was some kind of joke. But it wasn't. It obviously wasn't.

The brothers' faces—and the Hawks' beside them—contorted like someone had just thrust torches up their backsides.

So these five… Hawks think their people will bow to the commands of a vampire. Their species' arch-nemesis.

Now I found myself wondering whether the reason they'd given for why I alone had been scooped up by their "spies" was just a cock-and-bull story. A load of crap. I couldn't help but suspect that the Hawks had personally been spying on the area for a while, and saw their chance to pounce on me after the gas hit and I was vulnerable, when I would perhaps be more open to negotiation. It wouldn't have taken long for them to zoom down and get me. *There's always a hidden story with these creatures.*

I shifted on my feet, glancing once more toward the jungle—the direction where the IBSI was set up. My brother Lucas had left for The Shade to return with an army, but given the emptiness of the skies—and, frankly, the lack of noise—they clearly hadn't arrived yet. Or perhaps they had, but the smoke had prevented them from making any headway. Maybe it had even knocked a number of them unconscious, like it had done to the rest of us.

I refocused my attention on Killian. "So," I began, "you are telling me with a straight face that your people will bow to my command."

Killian nodded. "As I told you," he said, "we have heard of your exploits in other lands. We know what you are capable of. And you… you know far more about this new breed of hunters than we do."

Indeed, in theory, the Hawks should know practically nothing about them. The IBSI was an entirely different organization to the one Aiden had been a part of all those years ago. *The one these conniving Hawks had secretly been pulling the strings to.*

Drawing in a breath, I let them hang in suspense for about another minute. Finally, I replied, "All right. Since you have laid bare your incompetence and begged me, I will lead your people... But I have my conditions."

"What are they?" Killian asked tentatively.

I eyed him sternly. "First, before we do anything about the hunters, all five of you will fly with me over Aviary and help me find my missing family. Second, you must swear you and your people's full allegiance to me in battle. There will come a time in the very near future when I will call upon your help on Earth to assist in providing protection to humans from misbehaving supernaturals." Even as I spoke the words, I could hardly believe they'd uphold their word on this second condition. But even if they didn't, at least they would help find my family and rid their realm of the hunters. That was better than nothing. Besides, they should realize by now that it wasn't a good idea to tick off The Shadow League…

The five Hawks glanced at one another. It took less than a minute for Tidor and Killion to agree on their species' behalf.

"After we have searched for your family, we will require you to visit our residence to address our people," Killion said. "They will not stir, otherwise."

I nodded. "Naturally."

We didn't dally after that. Killian bowed for me to climb onto his back, and the five Hawks took off with me into the air. As we began soaring over the sprawling jungle landscape, the wind whipping through my hair, a part of me couldn't help but look forward to that meeting. To the role I was about to step up to.

I supposed it would become just another thing to add to my resume. Husband. Father. Grandfather. Vampire. Ex-human and fire-wielder. Ruler of The Shade. TSL Founder. And now… *Derek, King of Hawks?*

That suited me just fine…

Chapter 34: Grace

On returning to The Shade, Safi and I headed straight to the hospital where we assumed the rest of my family would be recovering from the fumes. The assumption was correct. We found them all resting in beds, most of them asleep, including my mother. Apparently, that smoke had drained them of energy, affected their brains in a way that just made them want to sleep. But Corrine informed me that they had already come to for a bit, and she was confident that they would all make a full recovery now that they were breathing clean air. Neither she nor any of the other witches and jinn were sure exactly what was in that smoke to make it toxic to even supernaturals.

Unable to greet my mother, I found myself wandering to the hospital room I had been staying in before we left. It was empty, I supposed still reserved for me.

I sat down on the mattress, my eyes wandering to the mirror fixed on the opposite wall. It was the first time I had looked at myself in hours and… God… I looked so much worse, it was frightening.

I tore my eyes away from the mirror, not wanting to keep track of the train wreck my body was quickly becoming. I found myself wondering just how slowly— or rather, rapidly—my transformation would keep creeping along. I could only be thankful for my fae blood. If I had been fully human, there would have been nothing stopping me from transforming right away. I would already be like Maura by now.

Would I keep getting sicker gradually, hour by hour, or would there come a breaking point when things would suddenly speed up, with very little warning of the final stage?

I lay back on the bed, my eyes glassy as I gazed up at

the ceiling. I let my vision cloud over.

Lawrence. I tried to block out thoughts about everything other than Lawrence. I tried to transport myself back to his room in Aviary, to the moment our lips had touched. To his hands on my waist. To the light scent of aftershave on his skin. I suspected that memory would become my sanctuary in the hours and days to follow… assuming I had days.

Someone rapped at the door. I glanced in its direction to see Orlando entering the room. He wore hospital pajamas. I wondered how long ago he'd woken up.

"Hey," he murmured.

He seated himself on the mattress next to me.

"You recovered already?" I asked, unable to muster neither the energy nor the will to sit up.

"I wouldn't say fully," he replied. "But as you can see, I'm walking. I woke up and heard from the jinn that you had returned… What happened with you? Did you find that guy?"

That guy. A small smile couldn't help but creep to my lips. "Yeah," I murmured, half in a dream. "I found that guy."

Orlando frowned. "So, what happened?"

"He agreed to help us," I replied. "He said that he will do everything he can to uncover the antidote and relay it to us."

"Well, that's good news," Orlando said, blowing out a breath. "But how long will it take?" His eyes moved nervously over me. "You're really not looking good, Grace."

"Yeah. I know. We've no idea how long it will take."

"I asked the witch already whether they'd made any progress in figuring out what's so special about those trees," Orlando said, looking down at his lap. "But they haven't had any luck so far. Apparently that warlock—Ibrahim—has a couple of Bloodless locked up in the place you call the Sanctuary."

I grimaced. *If Lawrence is too late, at least I'll have comrades...*

Orlando fell quiet for a while, which I was grateful for. I felt too emotionally drained and exhausted to hold a conversation with him right now. I couldn't even bring myself to feel awkward around him anymore. I was past all that.

"I guess I'll leave you to rest," he said finally, rising to his feet.

I didn't respond. I just looked at him, blankly.

He half twisted to the door, as if to move to it, but then conflict played across his face. Something was holding him back.

He cleared his throat, facing me fully again. "I… I said it before but I'll say it again. I'm sorry for kissing you earlier. It was really crappy timing and we should probably just pretend that it never happened." He paused, his chest constricting. "But… I do like you, Grace. Even though we haven't known each other long."

He gazed steadily at me.

I wasn't sure what he wanted me to say. That I liked him too? That I had fallen for him in the days we'd spent together?

The memory of Lawrence still seared fresh in my mind. I could practically still taste his lips on mine.

And yet I still wasn't sure how to respond to Orlando. Would I tell him, that I liked him too, but I already had a boyfriend? A lover? It felt like I had no such thing when I wasn't sure if I even had a life right now. I was clinging to the edge of a cliff, slipping closer and closer to a freefall with every minute that passed.

I felt in limbo. Like there was no point in even telling Orlando—or anyone—that I'd become infatuated with Lawrence, when it could all be so temporary. *Over before it even began.*

Instead I just gulped and nodded, acknowledging Orlando's compliment.

He nodded back stiffly, and then averted his eyes. He turned and left me alone in the room.

I sank back into my former dreamlike state, losing all sense of time and place. I was only vaguely aware of the witches and jinn wandering in and out every so often to check in on me. And I thought it was Safi who ended up taking a permanent seat in the corner of my room with a book. I remained lost in semi-consciousness.

Until I was roused by a nightmare.

The worst nightmare I'd experienced since leaving Chicago.

The tremors returned, as strong and forceful as ever. I began coughing again, spilling more blood.

But then something else happened.

Something terrifyingly new.

A tingling sensation erupted all over my skull and at the tips of my fingers and toes. The tingling turned into prickling, then stabbing, like somebody piercing me with needles.

Someone gripped my shoulders—Safi, I guessed—before a cry escaped my throat as the stabbing intensified. *Have I reached the final stage already? How many minutes or seconds do I have left of my life as me, Grace Novak? Will I leave before ever saying goodbye to my parents? To my family?*

Would I have any thoughts at all, on the other side? Would I even be aware of my actions? Would it be like dying?

The stabbing persisted along with the tremors for what felt like an eternity, but might have only been ten or twenty minutes. Then the shaking subsided. So did the stabbing.

Gasping in relief, I heaved myself into a sitting position. Safi and Corrine stood before me. I was expecting them to look as relieved as I felt, but found them staring at me with horror in their eyes. My gaze shooting to the mirror, I realized why.

Clumps of my hair had fallen out, leaving bare patches of pale scalp. My brown locks lay scattered all around my pillow. And my fingernails and toenails where the pain had been, although still attached, appeared... dislodged somehow. Loosened.

I trust you, Lawrence, and I think... I even love you. But short of you turning into Superman, it's going to be too late.

My time is drawing to a close.

Chapter 35: Victoria

I sat at the end of the jetty, gazing out at the ocean glistening beneath the moonlight. I'd spent the last few hours with my parents in the hospital, though they had been awake for only ten or twenty minutes before slipping back into exhaustion. My parents were vampires. I wasn't used to seeing them look so tired, so weary. It was disturbing. But Corrine said that it was simply the aftereffect of the toxic fumes they'd inhaled, and they would be back to normal soon. That I just needed to let them sleep it off. So I'd left them, along with the rest of my family, and ambled back out of the hospital.

My parents' abrupt return had temporarily pried my mind away from Bastien and the Mortclaws. But now, as I sat here in the quiet with nothing but my own thoughts for company, my anxiety returned full force.

I thought back to Mona's and my trip to the black witches' old island residence in the supernatural dimension. That green vial of liquid she had shown me.

The source of the Mortclaws' powers.

The witch had brought the elixir back with us to The Shade, and she was keeping it now safely stowed away in her spell room, out of my reach. She wouldn't even consider letting me near it again until I had talked to my parents about it.

I shuddered as I thought about Mona's "insane" idea. Before revealing it to me, she had asked me how much I truly wanted to be with Bastien.

And I found myself asking that question again now.

I knew that I loved him. And I knew that my love was deep. But what Mona had proposed would involve a whole new level of faith. Faith in Bastien. Faith in his and my relationship which, in spite of how true it felt, was still so very new. Both of us were still inexperienced.

Mona's idea *was* insane. Downright insane. It would involve me ingesting a drop of that green elixir—the product of a black ritual—in order to invoke a connection with the Mortclaws. A connection they could not deny, in spite of my being a human. She said it would form a bond that would make them feel instinctively drawn to me, as if I were of their own kind. This, according to Mona's knowledge of werewolf psychology, would make me more of a match for Bastien than Rona could ever be.

She said that I would also develop a kind of psychic connection with them, apparently one of the lesser-known powers of the Mortclaws. She suspected that I would be able to sense their location, as if attached to them by some long invisible string.

A single drop should not have any major effect on changing my constitution, who I was. Mona claimed that I would still look like myself, and I would not start shooting lasers from my eyes or sprout hair…

But even in spite of this, Mona continued to repeat a dozen times over that it was an extremely risky idea.

Extremely risky.

Even if everything worked according to plan, and I consumed just enough to convince them I was a worthy match for Bastien, I would still have the problem for the rest of my life of Brucella and the Northstones becoming my mortal enemies. Bastien had told me himself that a she-wolf like Brucella would never stop hunting me down, no matter what. In addition, once my decision was made and I'd consumed the liquid, there would be no going back. I would willingly become a member of the Mortclaw tribe, connecting myself to them, as they would be connected to me. They would gain an uncanny sense of my location, and I would never be truly free of them if things took a turn for the worst... Unless the vial was smashed. But I couldn't do that. Not without risking Bastien's safety—and maybe even, to a smaller extent, my own, if the magical liquid had ingrained itself even partially into my system. I didn't understand how such things worked. I was going blindly by Mona's words.

Proceeding with Mona's idea would be an utter leap of faith in the witch, but most of all, in Bastien and myself.

Hence, I realized that her question was the only one I needed to ask myself right now. The only thing I needed to consider... How much did I really want to be with that werewolf? How much did I really believe in our love? How much was I willing to give up for it?

After my parents had recovered, before even speaking a word to them about it, I had to answer these questions for myself. Gaining approval from my parents would be a whole other matter entirely. I couldn't even bring myself to think of the effort it would take just yet. And, although I was an adult, I didn't want to go through with this without it. It was far too big of a step.

I drew my legs up, pulling my knees against my chest, and leaned my chin against my kneecaps. I closed my eyes, letting the night breeze take me for a while, stilling my mind and listening to the peace that pervaded our island.

I tried to dig deep, deep inside me, as I mulled the question over and over.

How far am I willing to fall for love?

I wrapped my arms nervously around myself as a chill wind caught my hair.

Whatever my answer, I had to come up with it soon.

Epilogue: Bastien

I felt like an animal being led to slaughter as I returned to The Woodlands with the Mortclaws. My new *family*. My gut clenched at the word. Sendira and Vertus calling themselves my mother and father made me feel almost nauseated.

We arrived in a mountainous region of The Woodlands that I had rarely frequented, and that I hadn't even known was habitable. The pack led me through a hidden entrance behind a cluster of boulders—the entrance to an ancient tunnel. We entered and wound our way along it, moving deeper and deeper into the mountain. My mother claimed this was the mountain I had been born in. My old home.

On reaching the end of the tunnel, we arrived outside a rotting oaken door which led to a network of chambers and caves. We had no torches to cast light upon our path. We moved through the gloom by our night vision. My mother, grasping my hands, led me into a circular chamber that she explained was our old room. Coated with blankets of dust, it looked like it hadn't been entered for many, many years. A large bed took up most of the space, and at the end of it was a wooden cot, whose blankets lay upturned.

My mother led me to it and clasped the edges of the cot, her chest heaving. She turned to me with glistening eyes. "Bastien," she said in a soft voice, "here was the last time I saw you. Before you were taken from us… You were such a perfect, beautiful cub. Your clear eyes, shiny black fur… I still remember nursing you like it was yesterday." Her voice choking up, she approached me and wrapped her arms around me, planting a kiss on my cheek.

I sensed her warmth and affection for me, and I

wished that I could return it... but I felt cold inside. Empty. As much as I could not deny our innate connection, my soul was backing away.

How can I love someone who insists on holding me in chains? Who refuses to accept my love for someone other than the one she has ordained? Who refuses to open her mind to the possibility that my happiness is more important than her long-held traditions?

But I had gotten past trying to argue with her. I might as well argue with a rock.

When I didn't respond to her embrace, she pulled away. Melancholy infused her expression. "We will find each other again, Bastien," she said. "We will overcome the rift caused by all our years apart. You will understand me, your father and your family. And you will come to love Yuraya, deeply and truly. I promise."

I felt sick.

"Would you like some time alone?" she wondered. "Some time in our old room?"

I nodded. The *only* thing I wanted right now was to be alone.

I was relieved when she backed away to the door.

"Very well," she said. "In the meantime, we're going to go… out for a while."

I couldn't even bring myself to ask where as she exited, closing the door softly behind her. I gazed from the cradle to an old rocking chair in the opposite corner of the room. There were no windows in here through which I could gaze out at the sky to experience at least the illusion of being free. Just stifling darkness. I sank into the rocking chair, even as it creaked beneath my weight.

This room… This mountain… It was where I had started my life. Perhaps, if I had never been kidnapped, and never been taken away from the Mortclaw pack, I would be happy in this moment. I would be conditioned to their way of thinking. Perhaps, over the years, I would even have already fallen in love with Yuraya. But I could not rewrite history. I had grown up a Blackhall, and I had met Victoria. My past was a part of my being, and my mother expecting me to forget it and just start afresh… It was impossible.

I thought about my mother's threat—that if I ever saw Victoria again, they would not relent until they had tracked and hunted her down. That I had to forget about her, cast her from my mind, if I wanted her to remain safe. If I wanted her to remain *alive*.

Even if I had the ability to fly away from The Woodlands and make it back to The Shade on my own, I loved Victoria too much to put her in that kind of danger. I could not etch a black mark on her for the rest of her life, leave her with fear in her heart every time she stepped out of her island's proximity.

My mother had already scented Victoria, and even if we met for just a short while, she would detect Victoria's scent on me. The Mortclaws' senses were parallel to none.

I couldn't bring such a risk to Victoria. Which meant that my last memory of her—her standing in my room at the top of Blackhall mountain, covered by Aisha's protective halo—would be my last memory of her, ever.

I closed my eyes, recalling her terrified face, her cry as my mother had leapt toward me.

I wished that my last memory of her had been different than that. I wished that we had been alone. That my hands had been trailing through her hair, my lips claiming hers, before we whispered goodbyes.

But, again, I couldn't rewrite history.

I had to be content with the days and nights I'd had the privilege of spending with that sweet human girl. I supposed it was more than I had ever hoped for, anyway. I'd never expected love or romance out of life. It had been Victoria who had given rise to the realization such things even existed… and now that she was gone, I supposed that it was only fitting that they should vanish too.

And they would vanish. Even if, as my mother so confidently claimed, Yuraya was a perfect match for me, I would rather spend the rest of my life alone, cast adrift in the ocean. I would rather become a wanderer. A nomad, living on the memories and dreams I'd collected during the brief period when I had been free and in love.

That ought to be enough for me. My body might still hunger for Victoria, but that ought to be enough to feed my mind. I could spend the rest of my life in a fantasy, living what could have been. Anything was better than the reality my mother had chalked out for me.

Opening my eyes, I rose abruptly to my feet. I balled

my hands up into fists.

I have to get out of here. I have to run. Away. Far away.

Away from the watch of my family. Away from Yuraya's waiting arms...

Because if Victoria can't have me, nobody will.

***

I had no idea where I would go. My mother's sense for me was uncannily sharp. Maybe I would never fully escape her—maybe she would chase me to the ends of the world.

But that would not stop me from running.

I waited in the chamber until the sounds of werewolves retreating from the mountain faded. I could still detect a few wolves around, but... I couldn't wait any longer. I didn't know how long the rest would be gone for, and for all I knew, this could be as alone as I was ever going to get.

So, easing the door slowly open, I slipped out, my eyes wide and alert as I scanned the hallway. I headed down the route toward the exit, passing rooms and tunnels quickly, not daring to glance through any of the doorways. I moved like a shadow, silently, swiftly, until I reached the main exit.

"Bastien?" A voice spoke before I could pass through the main door.

I froze, twisting slowly to find Yuraya standing behind me. *Speak of the devil.* Her sleek black hair was braided, her bright green eyes sharp.

"You're still here," I murmured, my throat dry.

"I… I hoped to catch you alone," she replied.

Without warning, she strode forward. The next thing I knew, she was gripping my right hand. She raised it to her mouth and planted a moist kiss on the back of it.

Disgusted, I jerked my hand away and staggered back.

A smile curved her lips. "Don't be shy, Bastien," she said. "I won't bite… Our bonding rituals will begin tomorrow, and we will be sharing a bed within a week… You might as well start getting used to me."

Horror surging within me, I whirled around and raced away, even as she called, "Where are you going?" My pounding footsteps echoed off the walls as I sped toward the opening of the mountain.

I assumed my wolf form the moment I burst out into

the open. Landing on all fours, I hurtled away from the mountain and into the nearest line of trees. I ran, gathering all the speed my limbs could muster, whizzing through the forest in a blur.

I tried to lose myself in my speed, as I had done the night the hunters had struck Rock Hall. The night I'd thought that Victoria had betrayed me.

I ran and ran, unsure of where I was going. I could only think that I needed to reach the shore. A boat. Or maybe just leap into the ocean again, despite its dangers. The water would mask my scent better.

I would never have stopped—not once—until I reached the coast, if the sound of howling had not pierced the night. Howls so anguished, I stalled. My ears perked up. It sounded like the howls were coming from the East. In a daze of confusion, I couldn't help but be drawn toward the sound. I hadn't heard such cries since the night the hunters invaded. My pulse raced, and a part of me feared that they might have even returned somehow to exact revenge.

I sped for miles, the howls growing louder and louder, and then I realized... I was racing toward the

Northstones' lair. I pushed myself faster still, until I burst forth from the trees into the glade outside the Northstones' mountain home.

For a split second as I gazed upon the scene before me, I thought I was witnessing a battle. But I quickly realized that it was a massacre. A bloody massacre. The Mortclaws, in their giant black wolf forms, were dragging members of the Northstones from the entrance of their abode out onto the glade where they ripped them apart. I almost yelled as I realized not only were they murdering them—tearing through their necks with their teeth, and into their stomachs with their razor-sharp claws—they were *eating* them. Just as I had witnessed them do to Brucella,

They were killing the Northstones for food.

I had prayed with all that I had that the Mortclaws had eaten Brucella only because they had been desperate, because there had been nothing else edible on that ghastly island. But The Woodlands was a verdant land filled with food for wolves.

The Mortclaws were cannibals, through and through.

I choked as I caught sight of my father grabbing hold

of Sergius, who was attempting—pathetically—to fight back. Sergius and I had never been very close. But I'd grown up calling him Uncle, and he was never abominable to me. If it weren't for his wife, I was sure that we would have been closer.

My desire to remain hidden from the Mortclaws completely vanishing from my mind, I hurtled toward my father, my teeth bared. Although I wasn't nearly as large as him, the force of my colliding into his side made him stagger, and as he realized it was me, he dropped Sergius. But, from the amount of blood that was gushing from Sergius' neck, it was obvious that he was already as good as gone.

"What are you doing?" I roared, panic and desperation gripping me.

My father, apparently mad with hunger, averted his attention from me and scooped up Sergius again.

"No!" I bellowed.

"Bastien!" my mother called behind me.

I turned to see her mouth dripping with blood. Whose blood, exactly, I didn't want to imagine.

"We must eat, child," she scolded, as if I was the

unreasonable one. "We have been starved for decades!"

"But there are plenty of—"

My voice trailed off as a female wolf cried, "Father! No!" Then came a stifled howl.

My eyes darting to the direction of the voice, I realized that it was Rona. She had come speeding from a hidden side of the mountain toward her father... only to be quickly caught by one of the younger males of the Mortclaw pack.

My mother had already lost interest in me by now— her attention span matched my father's, it seemed, when it came to the warm flesh of their own kind. She darted toward a fallen corpse and continued eating, while I zoomed in on the male wolf dragging Rona toward an emptier area where I knew he was about to rip her open. I leapt forward. Reaching him, I managed to blindside him, causing him to stagger aside. Infuriated, he whirled on me... but on seeing who I was, he reined himself in. With a frustrated growl, he retreated.

Gripping the back of Rona's neck between my teeth, I tugged on her, indicating that she follow me through the trees. The ground squelched with blood; the glade had become a red marshland. Droplets soiled my legs and underbelly as I raced away from the clearing and back into the forest with Rona. We kept running until the clearing was out of sight.

Then I paused as Rona fell behind, my limbs quivering from the shock and trauma of what I'd just witnessed.

Rona struggled to run any further as she broke down. "My father!" she rasped.

"If you want to stand a chance of living, you have to keep up with me," I growled.

She forced herself onward, bounding alongside me with uneven footing. As we moved away from The Northstones' lair, the howls grew less and less. Not from the distance we'd put between us and them—I imagined every one of them had been felled by now as the Mortclaws relished their midnight feast.

I'd never had a nightmare as abhorrent as this.

My life has become worse than a nightmare.

I kept glancing over my shoulder, fearing I'd glimpse the Mortclaws chasing after us as we moved closer and closer to the ocean. All the while, I had to continue blasting Rona—who, I reminded myself, was *not* actually my cousin—to keep her from giving up.

Finally, a salty breeze trickled through the thinning trees and filled our nostrils. We arrived at the shore, bounding out onto the sand.

Rona collapsed, surrendering to her grief.

And I... I wasn't sure what to think, or what to do now. My only objective just a matter of hours ago had been to flee The Woodlands. Find somewhere within the universe where I could seek refuge from the life that had been dealt to me.

But now... How could I abandon my homeland now?

The Mortclaws were not merely killing the Northstones out of revenge. They were killing to *eat*. For *food*. My mother had said so herself.

In which case, what if the Northstones were only the beginning of the Mortclaws' attacks?

Who would be next? The Blackhall tribe? What of Cecil, and the others I loved?

I'd never felt so powerless. I was as good as a stranger to my parents and so-called family while they were in the heat of their hunger. They were far too strong for me to overcome even one of them, let alone take on all of them. And whom among my compatriots could I call upon to help? It wasn't like I could gather an army to quell them. They would simply become the next targets of the Mortclaws' appetite. Being the leaders' son, I was safe.

But what chance did everyone else stand?

Gods help The Woodlands.

READY FOR THE NEXT PART OF THE NOVAK CLAN'S STORY?

Dearest Shaddict,

The next book in the series is *A Shade of Vampire 30: A Game of Risk!* *A Game of Risk* releases **July 14th, 2016. Don't miss it!**

Visit **www.bellaforrest.net** for details.

Here's a preview of the awesome cover:

Thank you for reading, and I will see you again very soon!

Love,

Bella xxx

P.S. Join my VIP email list and I'll send you a personal reminder as soon as I have a new book out. Visit here to sign up: **www.forrestbooks.com**

(You'll also be the first to receive news about movies/TV show as well as other exciting projects that may be coming up!)

P.P.S. Follow The Shade on Instagram and check out some of the beautiful graphics: @ashadeofvampire

You can also come say hi on Facebook: www.facebook.com/AShadeOfVampire

And Twitter: @ashadeofvampire

CPSIA information can be obtained
at www.ICGtesting.com
Printed in the USA
LVOW03s2138160917
548993LV00002B/21/P